Keep It Secret

Sam Vickery

Copyright © 2018 Sam Vickery

First published worldwide 2018

All characters and events in this publication are fictitious and any resemblance to real persons, living or dead is purely coincidental.

All rights reserved.

No part of this publication may be reproduced, stored in a retrieval system or transmitted, in any form or by any means, without the prior permission in writing of the author.

www.samvickery.com

Mum, this one is for you.
For reading all my books, for loving me and for being you.

The Gratitude Page

Thank you so much to everyone who has helped to bring this book into the world. I want to give special thanks to my incredible Beta and ARC teams, who are the first people that get to read my stories and feedback to me on them. I never ever feel nervous sharing my words, knowing that you will be kind, constructive and giddy with excitement to read my books.

To my fantastic cover designer, Stuart Bache, thank you for coming up with such a perfect design to fit the story. I think it speaks for itself and it's been wonderful working with you.

To Bryan Cohen and his team who came up with the punchy book description that fits the story perfectly, thank you so much for all your hard work and patience with me!

To all of my wonderful readers who have supported me so far, buying and reviewing my books, commenting and emailing to ask when the next one is coming out, this is for you! I hope it's worth the wait and I appreciate every single one of you. Writing is my passion and the fact that you keep reading my stories makes me unbelievably happy.

And finally, to my family. My wonderful husband, Jed and my darling children, thank you for letting me work, for giving me time and for inspiring me to keep creating.

"A mother's love for her child is like nothing else in the world. It knows no law, no pity. It dares all things and crushes down remorselessly all that stands in its path."

Agatha Christie

Chapter One

There was a dead body on my kitchen floor. My mind should have been spinning, panicked, and yet it was more quiet than it had ever been. I glanced at the ticking clock, realising that Sophie must be getting hungry by now, it was past her dinner time. Straining my ears, I heard the comforting sounds of her singing to her dolls, the sweet lullaby of a girl who was made for motherhood, a child who has learned to nurture in spite of her own experience. She wouldn't come down until I called her. Even after two years, I knew she couldn't let go of those ingrained habits. She would wait, quietly, patiently, until she knew I was ready for her.

I looked at the motionless form sprawled on his back across the once sparkling white tiles, a pool of blood collecting in the creases of his arms, beneath his neck. He was wearing a thick gold chain that looked almost comical on his skinny frame, like some sort of cartoon gangster, and there was a tattoo of a skull peeking out from beneath the crusting blood that ran across his scrawny bicep. I twisted my mouth, staring at him, my eyes travelling over the brownish red puddle on my floor. I hoped it wouldn't leave a stain.

The thought struck me as cold, heartless and I shivered, the shock seeming to hit me all at once. Just a few hours before, I had been picking Sophie up from the school gates, my arms wrapping around her small waist, her hand slipping into mine as her words rushed out, telling me all about who she'd played with at lunch, the drawing she'd done of a baby elephant which she'd decorated with real leaves and grass collected from the school field. We'd stopped at the park on the way home, laughing as we'd swung side by side, challenging each other to go higher until it had felt like we were flying.

And now... now I had a body in my house. Blood on my floor. The bile rose in my throat before I knew it was coming. I span, grasping for the counter, heaving blindly into the chunky ceramic of the Belfast sink until there was nothing left inside me. Disgusted with myself for losing control, I rinsed away the evidence of my shock, letting the tap run boiling hot until the sink was clean. I straightened up, grabbing a bottle of bleach from the cupboard, pouring it liberally into the basin, scrubbing and rinsing until I could no longer smell the contents of my stomach.

I glanced at the pool of blood, wondering briefly if I should clean it now too, but I shook the thought away. That would make it look like I'd tampered with evidence. Like I was trying to cover up what

I'd done. Hide something. It would look like a murder scene, and that was not something I could risk. I would have to be patient, difficult as it may be. The metallic smell of blood was strong enough to break through the fumes of the bleach and I was itching to pick up a cloth.

I dragged my eyes away from the body as I strode past it into the hall, my heels clicking against the tiles as I looked straight ahead. I dipped my hand inside my deep leather handbag, fumbling around before yanking out my lipstick, reapplying it with shaking hands in the hallway mirror. It was only then that I saw it. A streak of claret smeared across my forearm, the edges already flaking and brown. My stomach lurched heavily again, but this time I managed to swallow down my disgust. I took a breath, and then another, meeting my reflection in the mirror. "Get a grip, Isabel. Sophie needs you to be strong." I stared back at myself seeing the determination in my bright green eyes, the hard set of my mouth as I prepared to do what was necessary. And then I picked up my mobile phone and dialled 999.

Chapter Two

The second I ended the call, I knew I'd made a mistake. The police were going to come, and quickly. I'd be lucky if I had five minutes and then the house would be swarming. They might insist I come to the station. They might even arrest me. In fact, as I thought about it more clearly now, I realised they probably would. It didn't matter how I explained it, the fact remained that there was a dead body in my house and they needed someone to blame. I couldn't risk them taking Sophie. The phone was back in my hands before I finished the thought. It rang shrilly as I tapped my foot impatiently on the floor, biting my lip until I tasted blood.

"Hello?" came the deep voice as he finally

answered.

"Lucas," I breathed. "You have to come. You have to come here now."

"Isabel?"

"Now, Lucas. I need you to come for Sophie. Before they do."

"Before who do, Issy? You aren't making any sense – "

"I don't have time to explain, please, just come okay?"

"I'm coming. Oscar, get your jumper on, we're going out," he called, his voice muffling for a moment.

"No. No jumper, Lucas. I'm not joking, there is no time. Just come. Now!" I ended the call, slamming down the phone and ran upstairs, pushing open Sophie's bedroom door. It was the lightest room in the house, south facing and decorated in soft creams and yellows. Her bedspread was covered in tiny butterflies and the wall beside her bed had been transformed into a secret garden, with huge transfers of trees, flowers and yet more butterflies. The massive window was perfectly placed to let in the maximum amount of sunshine. Sophie sat in the middle of the thick cream carpet, her dolls laid out carefully on blankets and makeshift beds. They were all in varying states of undress. She was sealing the sticky tabs on a tiny nappy, her tongue poked out between her rosebud mouth as she concentrated on the task. Wordlessly I walked towards her, squatting down and clearing my throat to get her attention. It would have felt more natural to touch her on the shoulder or to put my arm around her, but I knew she still startled easily and I hated to frighten her.

She looked up at me with a wide, trusting smile. "Hi, Mummy! Look at what my baby can do!" She finished putting the nappy on the bald baby doll, then moved towards another one. This one had wild auburn hair and porcelain skin. "Just like you, Mummy!" Sophie had exclaimed when she'd seen it in the toy shop. It had been one of the first times I'd seen her face light up with pure joy like that, and I'd bought it for her without hesitation. She'd named it Belle, after me she said, though nobody ever called me that. Not anymore. Sophie picked the baby doll up as carefully as you would a newborn child, her arm naturally moving to support her curly head. She twisted, placing her onto the tiny pink plastic potty. After a few seconds, she lifted her back into her arms. "Look, she did a wee, Mummy!"

"Oh, wow! I didn't know she could do that."

"Joanna showed me her one at school. You have to give her a drink of water in her bottle. I can't believe we didn't know, look Mummy, do you see? It's really there!"

"I see it. What a clever baby," I said, forcing

myself to smile at her. "Darling, Uncle Lucas is on his way to pick you up. You're going to have dinner with him and Oscar tonight. And actually," I added as an afterthought, "you and Oscar can have a sleepover. Won't that be fun?" I grinned, already tossing pyjamas and clean underwear into her unicorn backpack.

Sophie screwed up her face. "Do I have to? I wanted you to read the next chapter of The Faraway Tree to me. It's *The land of Do-As-You-Please* tonight!" I held out my hand and she took it, getting to her feet.

"I'll put it in your bag and Uncle Lucas can read it at bedtime, okay? Oscar will like it too, I'm sure."

"Okay," she agreed. "I like when he reads stories. He always makes them funny."

"Good." I guided her towards the stairs, feeling relieved that she wasn't going to make a scene. She'd stayed with Lucas and Oscar before, but there were times she couldn't bear to leave me, times when she just needed me to stay close. Thankfully, this wasn't going to turn into one of them. I pushed her feet into her sandals and opened the front door, stepping outside. I was relieved to see Lucas running up the driveway, Oscar grinning as he jogged along beside him. I pushed the ridiculous backpack into Lucas's chest, glancing nervously up the road.

"What's going on, Issy?" he asked, his big dark eyes penetrating mine, searching for answers. He was the tallest man I'd ever met, huge and bearlike, but I'd never felt afraid of him. I knew I could trust him with my life. With my daughter's life.

"I haven't got time to explain," I said, leaning down to kiss Sophie. I could hear the unmistakable sound of sirens now, they were approaching fast. "Can she stay over? She hasn't eaten and she has her book in her bag and – "

Oscar gave a squeal of delight and I balled my hands into fists as I followed his gaze. Rounding the corner at full speed were two police cars, lights flashing, the sound of the sirens almost deafening. They skidded to a halt on the kerb outside my house, closely followed by a third police car and a van. The sight of so many of them was overwhelming.

"Issy – "

"Take the children. Now." My voice was calm and steady, but I felt the tremble in my lips as I spoke.

"What the hell is going on, Isabel?"

"Lucas... Please!" I begged. The police were pouring out of their vehicles now, making their way up the driveway towards us.

"Mummy, what do they want?" Sophie said, tugging at my wrist, her eyes uncertain. I hated the fear in them. I wished I could take it away.

"They just need my help with something. It's good to help the police, isn't it, darling?" She nodded though she didn't let go of me.

"Lucas," I said again, this time more sharply than I'd intended. He stared at me, his face creased in worry. And then he gave a nod. "Come on kids. Let's go." He scooped Sophie into his arms, and grabbed Oscar by the hand.

"But, Dad!"

"No, Oscar. This isn't the time." He turned toward the road, pulling a disgruntled Oscar behind him. "Call me. The moment you can."

I nodded. Then I turned to face the uniformed officers. "You had better come inside."

Chapter Three

The whole situation was more surreal than I could handle. It felt wrong to treat these men and women in uniform as guests, given the reason for their arrival. Yet I couldn't seem to cast aside my manners. I almost offered round tea and coffee before I caught myself, swallowing the words back down, knowing that I'd seem like a lunatic. I needed them to know I was sane. A professional woman, who happened to be caught in the wrong place at the wrong time. They had to know that I was the victim here despite the horror of what they would find on my kitchen floor. But still, it didn't feel right to have them in my home and not offer them a drink and a seat.

I've been told by just about everyone that I'm a

good host. Fantastic actually. That I have the ability to make people feel utterly taken care of, yet relaxed enough that they could be in their own home. The perfect balance apparently. It is not, as my colleagues and the mums from Sophie's school like to assume, a natural proclivity for entertaining. It's a skill I've created, devised as part of a complex and relentless pretence. The story I need people to believe about me. I have studied obsessively those women who always seem to have their lives in order. The smiling, happy, confident women who never get stressed or flustered. I've emulated the soft, calm tones of their voices, mirrored their style, learnt the way they run their homes, the food they serve at dinner parties, the topics they pick for conversation. I've made countless mistakes, but I never gave up. I strived to do better, knowing how important it was for me to be accepted.

I *have* to be the kind of person that others want

to be around. Someone they can trust with their secrets, share their problems with and invite to help solve them. I *have to* be given the opportunity to make lives better, to give love to those who need it. To be thought of as a good person. Because if I'm her, if I'm Isabel Cormack, the woman with the fantastic hosting skills, the selfless single woman who gave up her freedom to adopt that little girl, the sister who can always be relied upon to make the sensible choice, and who never says no, if I'm her, then I won't be me. If I pretend hard enough, then maybe I'll even forget the truth one day. Maybe I'll even believe I'm as good as I let everyone think.

I scanned the group of police who were traipsing into the hall behind me and did a quick head count. There were actually only eight of them, six men and two women, but if you'd asked me two minutes before I'd have guessed closer to twenty. The instinct to introduce myself was forcing its way up,

I felt like I should have been holding out my hand, making eye contact with each of them, remembering every name, but there was no time for any niceties. One officer, a grey haired man with beefy arms and a no nonsense expression on his lined face, stepped forward, his words coming briskly.

"Isabel Cormack? You rang 999 and reported an incident, correct?" I nodded. "An intruder?" I nodded again, my eyes flicking towards the closed kitchen door. The rest of the group were already fanning out, two heading for the stairs, three for the living room. And two were making their way down the hall towards the kitchen.

"Wait!"

They stopped, all of them staring at me. The grey haired officer frowned. "Did he go out the front?"

I shook my head. "I wasn't... I d-didn't expect so many of you to come – "

"There's been a spate of burglaries in the area. We're keen to catch the culprits, so if we could just hurry this along, Miss Cormack?" he said pointedly. "Which way did he escape?"

I stared up at him, feeling the dizzying thump of my heart. My breath was catching on a lump that had formed in my throat, it felt like it was slowly closing, like soon I wouldn't be able to draw in air at all. Like the world was closing in on me and I had no way to escape, nowhere to run. I shouldn't have called them. I should have done things differently, I should have thought this through before I brought them here. I could see the impatience on his face as he waited for me to speak. "Front or back, Miss Cormack?"

I shook my head. "He's... he's in there," I pointed, my finger trembling, the reality of my situation hitting me. He glanced to the duo nearest the kitchen door, giving them a nod. "Go. All of you."

I reached for his arm, panic coursing through me, my palm slick with sweat as I grasped the sleeve of his pressed uniform. "You have to understand. I had no choice. He gave me no choice. I didn't mean for..."

The door was thrust open, seven pairs of feet thundering through the house, deafening as they ran. "Oh my god!" one of the women shouted. There was a static sound as she got on her radio, and I heard her tell someone to send an ambulance immediately.

"Drew, get in here!" someone else shouted. He didn't hesitate as he yanked his arm from my grip, spinning on his heel and storming into the kitchen after his colleagues, leaving me standing alone. I felt my knees buckle and then I was sliding to the ground, my back hitting the cold metal of the radiator, my arms wrapping around my knees as if I could make myself small enough to disappear.

"He gave me no choice," I whispered. "He gave me no choice."

Chapter Four

I'd been arrested. I'd known it was a possibility, but now that it had really happened I was struggling to keep calm. Twice on the short journey from my house to the St Aldates police station in central Oxford, I'd glanced down at my handcuffed wrists and felt myself spiralling into a panic attack. My chest tightening, my heart pounding erratically, my breathing coming in sharp shallow bursts. I was consumed with an overwhelming need to get out of the car by any means possible, to escape and get back to my child. To run where we could never be found. Somehow though, I had managed to pull myself back from the frenzied panic and grasp onto that last thin strand of self control. I couldn't let myself fall apart. Not yet.

Now, I sat in the boxy interview room, my sweating palms clasped around a polystyrene cup of lukewarm tea the colour of dishwater, the murmur of passing voices outside in the hall as I waited alone. I didn't know how long they would leave me here to stew. It could be minutes or a lot longer. What I *was* sure of though, was that the instant that door opened, the questions would begin. I had to know exactly what I was going to say, how to make them understand. I had to be prepared. The tea remained undrunk between my palms as my mind whirred, my thoughts flicking like a catalogue of options as I went over every single path, every little way I could tell my story so they would believe me, feel sorry for me even. *I* was the victim here.

The door opened and I looked up, expecting to see the steely face of the constable who'd grilled me at my house. Instead there were two people I hadn't met before. A man and a woman, both smartly dressed in plain clothes. They approached briskly, taking their seats across the table from me, and the woman placed a thin file on the table, meeting my eyes. She was petite, a sharp chestnut coloured bob shining under the glare of the strip lighting, a simple gold band on her ring finger. The man was a little younger than her, perhaps thirty five or so. His dark hair was clipped short and he had sweat marks under his armpits. He had wiry black hair curling from beneath the sleeves of his blue shirt, travelling over the backs of his hands, almost to his fingers. He saw me looking and I tore my gaze away, staring down at my tea.

"Good evening, Miss Cormack," the woman said in a clear, strong voice. "I'm DCS Robbins, this is DCI Barnes." I watched out of the corner of my eye as he pressed a button on a tape recorder, wondering why they didn't have something more modern in place. It was 2018 and they were still using tech from my childhood. DCS Robbins reeled off a spiel that brought back memories of watching The Bill with my twin sister, Bonnie, stating all of our names and the time and date, and then gave me a cool smile. "So, Miss Cormack – "

"It's Isabel," I said softly.

"Isabel then. Tell me what happened."

"I... I'm not sure where to begin..."

She nodded, clearly expecting my response. "Okay. Why don't you tell me about your relationship with the man we found at your home today? Did you know him well?"

I shook my head, meeting her eyes. "No, not well. Not at all really. He's a decorator, a handyman. I got a leaflet through the door a couple of months back. I still have it, I think."

"So, he's been working for you?"

"Just the past two weeks. I needed some work done at home, plastering and tiling in the bathroom.

I remembered his leaflet, so I called him. I've barely spoken to him though, he always came in when I was at work, and my daughter was at school. I didn't want her disrupted by the work."

"I see. It says here a man was with you when the police arrived. He then left with two children. Was he at your home during this incident?"

"No, oh no, he wasn't. Sophie, my daughter, was upstairs but when I called you I knew she needed to get out of the house. I didn't want her to be frightened, so I called Lucas. He's my brother-in-law. He only lives across the road from me, literally two minutes away. I told him to come and get her."

"Did he come inside?"

I shook my head.

"Out loud please, Isabel."

"No. He only arrived a minute before the police came. I took Sophie out to meet him."

"And he's your sister's husband?"

"He was..." I sighed. "He's widowed. Roxy died six years ago. She had a brain tumour."

"I'm sorry," she said, her words filled with feeling. I nodded, swallowing. "So, what happened with the handyman? Did you have a disagreement?"

"No, nothing like that." I took a sip of the stone cold tea, buying time. It was imperative that they believed me now. I placed the cup down on the table, hiding my shaking hands in my lap. "He finished the work a few days ago. I'd paid him. As far as I was concerned, I wouldn't see him again. But this evening..." I bit my lip. "I picked Sophie up from school. We went to the park, and then when we got home, she went upstairs to play while I stayed in the kitchen to get dinner sorted. It's what we do every night. I was just washing up the breakfast things – I don't always have time in the mornings," I shrugged apologetically. "He must have got a key cut before he finished the job. I didn't hear him come in..."

"Why would he come back? Surely he expected you to be there?"

I shook my head. "No. I wasn't supposed to be there. I had planned to go camping with Sophie in the New Forest. It's half term next week. I'd planned to take her straight from school and spend the week there."

"And you think he knew that?"

"I know he did. He recommended the campsite to me."

"But you didn't go?"

"I changed my mind. The weather said it would be raining a lot, and I'm not an experienced camper. And then this afternoon I saw a poster for the circus. It's only going to be here for the week and I knew Sophie would love it. She loves the acrobats." I gave a small shrug, my fingernails digging into my palms, hidden beneath the table. "He must have assumed the house would be empty."

"So you surprised him?"

"He surprised me. At first I thought he must have left something behind when he finished the job. But then I saw, he was holding my mother's vase, and the locked box where I keep money for the food shopping and Sophie's school trips. There wasn't much cash in there, but the vase is worth a lot. He knew that too because I'd warned him to be careful of it when he brought in his ladder, then I'd put it away in a cupboard. Told him I couldn't risk it being broken. It was stupid of me."

"How did you react when you saw him with it?" DCS Robbins said, steepling her fingers beneath her chin.

"I told him to put down my things and get out. He put down the cash-box and I thought he was going to listen to me, but then, he pulled out a screwdriver," I whispered. My hands had migrated from my lap, my fingernails tapping quickly against the thick polystyrene cup. "He came right at me with it. My daughter was upstairs... alone... and... and..." I realised I was crying, fat tears splashing down my cheeks, hitting the scratched wooden surface of the table. DCS Robbins pushed a box of tissues towards me, her eyes softening.

"And what, Isabel?"

"It all happened so fast. I didn't think, not really. I grabbed the knife off the draining board and... and I stabbed him. I didn't mean to... I was just so scared. He was going to kill me, I know he was." I looked up at the two of them with a pleading expression and I saw the sympathy written on their faces. "I had no choice. It was my home, *my home* and he was going to kill me for a vase! It was self defence. I would never hurt someone on purpose, never," I sobbed. I was crying hysterically now, struggling to catch my breath as the reality of what

I'd done washed over me. "Is he... did he make it?" I asked through a veil of tears. But I already knew the answer.

"No, Isabel. David Harrison is dead."

Chapter Five

Despite the fact that Summer was barely over, the police station was already blasting out the central heating at full pelt. It had been 18°C in the park last week. I'd worn a short skirt with no tights and Sophie had run around in a cotton dress and flip flops. October wasn't winter, and we were in the midst of a heat wave, but I doubted they cared here. They were probably just trying to protect themselves from being sued if someone developed pneumonia in one of their cells. And these days, I expected that wasn't too far from the reality.

Despite the stuffy, oppressive heat of my tiny cell, I found that I couldn't stop trembling. I sat as still as I possibly could, convinced that I was being watched over the grainy CCTV, trying to look calm on the outside, while the flood of emotions I'd been trying to stem all night raged through me. Memories I could no longer squash down flashed through my mind. Thoughts that I'd been sure were locked away in boxes, never to emerge, flitted like an old film across the canvas of my mind, muddying it, distorting everything.

I couldn't work out how long I'd been locked up – there were no windows in the cell, no natural light to give me a clue of the time, but there had been a period where the overhead lights had been dimmed, not to the point of real darkness, but enough to give the illusion of night-time.

Now they were bright and obnoxious as they glared down from above. I hadn't slept. I'd been sitting for hours perched on the edge of the hard, uncomfortable bed, my cold bare feet numb against the concrete floor. They had confiscated my stilettos. Said they were prohibited, could be considered a weapon. It had taken all my willpower to quietly hand them over without an argument. How could I explain to them that I needed those shoes? That they were a part of who I was. The mask of the well dressed, perfectly made up woman I chose to present to the world. When you started to strip away all of my armour, I ran the risk of being seen for what I really was. And I could never let that happen. Not now. I was a mother, I had a child to protect. I would not let them see.

My head pounded with the strain of thinking so hard, memories I wanted to erase. I felt like my brain might combust under the pressure. I'd killed a man. Taken his life. He would never see another sunrise, never feel joy or fear or love again. He was gone. I tried to work out what that meant for me. Who had I become? Can a single action change who you are, or is it only a build-up of actions – or inactions, that shape a person? I didn't have an answer for that. Not yet. But as I sat wishing I could call out, ask for a blanket or two to cocoon myself against the persistent trembling, yet knowing I couldn't without drawing unwanted attention to myself, I was sure of one thing. Put in the same situation again, I wouldn't change what I'd done. I would kill him again.

Chapter Six

It was possible to work out the length of time I'd been a prisoner by the quantity and composition of the meals I was given. There had been the cold, undercooked toast and rubbery microwaved scrambled eggs about an hour after the lights had come up. A biscuit and a cup of tea arrived a few hours later. This been followed by a room temperature cheese sandwich, curling at the edges, accompanied by a cup of vegetable soup, and finally a tray with some sort of creamy tuna pasta combo and a sugar free yoghurt. I'd left all of it untouched, unable to even fathom how they could expect me to eat in these circumstances. It had taken all of my strength not to vomit at the smell alone.

At some point between the lunch and dinner

offerings, I'd finally been allowed to make a phone call. Lucas had bombarded me with questions and I'd had to tell him I didn't have answers to any of them. I didn't know what was going to happen to me. I'd been told nothing since my emotional confession the previous night and I was feeling more and more certain by the minute that they were intentionally trying to make me feel panicky and skittish, so that I might suddenly blurt out some other snippet of information they could use to their advantage. The idea that I might not make it home to Sophie, that I would let her down, forced me to keep calm. I could not lose my cool, not even for a second.

When Lucas had put her on the phone, I'd held it so tight I thought it might crack, my palms shaking with the need to be close to her. "Hi darling, are you okay?"

"Yes, Mummy. Oscar wouldn't let me play with

his spaceship though. He said I would break it, but I won't, will I?"

"Was it the Lego one, sweetie?"

"Uh hu."

"Oh dear. You remember how proud Oscar is of those models? I'm sure he trusts you, he's just scared. Did you find something else to play with?"

"Yes, and I showed Uncle Lucas how Belle can do a wee!" she giggled.

"Good."

"When are you coming home, Mummy? Soon?"

I didn't miss the note of hopefulness in her sweet voice. "I'm not sure, there's a lot of work to be done here."

"Are you a police woman now then?"

"No, not really, sweetie, I'm just giving them some help. You know how mummy has to help the police for my job sometimes?"

"Like you did when you found me?"

I swallowed, forcing myself not to give in to tears. "Yes, Sophie. A bit like that."

There was a beat of silence and then her tiny voice crackled as she tried to put the pieces together. "Oh... does that mean... will you be bringing another little girl or boy home?"

I shook my head, feeling the wetness behind my eyes, blinking it back with stubborn determination. "No darling, that's not what I'm doing. It's nothing like that. Don't you worry, I'll be back with you really soon okay?"

"Okay, Mummy."

"I love you."

"I love you too."

The joy at hearing Sophie's voice had kept me sane for the rest of the afternoon, but slowly the memory of our conversation had ebbed away, until I'd found myself lost in fear and a tangle of never-ending questions all over again. The exhaustion was starting to make me dizzy, the bare walls of the cell seeming to bend and distort, my vision becoming blurred after a day and a half awake. But there was no way I could rest. I pushed the heels of my hands into my eye sockets, rubbing ferociously, desperately trying to eliminate the sea of black spots that danced in the air in front of me.

There was a sudden sound of metal on metal as the heavy bolt of my cell door slid back, and a police officer I didn't recognise stepped inside. "Follow me please, Miss Cormack." He stood patiently as I clambered to my feet, blinking away the head-rush, trying to ignore the sudden drum-roll of my heart pounding against my ribcage. I'd been so keen to know what was happening with the investigation, I hadn't thought about how hard it would be when the time came for them to make a decision. Was I walking towards my freedom, or would I be kept here, locked up like a wild animal waiting to be put down? I was led into the very same interview room where I'd waited last night, only this time DCS Robbins and DCI Barnes were already waiting. He'd changed his shirt, but I could see there were huge patches of wetness beneath the armpits once again, the green cotton darker than the rest. Was it nerves or was he just a perpetually sweaty man? Or maybe it was just the overwhelming heat of the station combined with cheap, ineffective antiperspirant.

"Please take a seat," DCI Barnes instructed. I did as he said, concentrating on not fidgeting as I waited for them to be the first to break the silence.

"We're sorry to keep you waiting for so long, Isabel," DCS Robbins said. "As I'm sure you can understand, we had to gather evidence and look into the incident. I can tell you it makes our jobs much easier when we are given the truth of the matter up front." I bit the inside of my cheek, not daring to say a word. Was she thanking me or accusing me? "Mr Harrison's body was searched and a key was found matching the lock to your front door. We had it confirmed this evening that he had it cut in town two weeks ago, and his fingerprints were all over it."

I nodded. "Oh."

My team have also corroborated your story. There was a cash box on the kitchen side, which also had his fingerprints on, and the vase you mentioned was smashed on the kitchen floor.

"He dropped it when... when I – " I couldn't finish the sentence.

"When you stabbed him," she finished the sentence for me. "Yes, that was the conclusion of the forensics team too."

"What will happen to me now?"

"You've been through a frightening experience, Isabel. Mr Harrison was an intruder in your home, and the law says that you have a right to defend yourself if you feel threatened. We found a single stab wound to the chest, and it seems he was killed instantly. I'm sure your intention was simply to buy time, not to cause his death, but that's the risk you take if you break into a person's house. You defended yourself in your own home, and that is not considered a crime in this country."

"So... you aren't going to charge me?"

"No. You're free to go."

"Really?"

"Yes, Isabel," she smiled gently. "Go home to your daughter. We'll be in touch if we need any further information from you. And make sure you have all your locks changed first thing tomorrow, okay?"

"Yes... yes I will. Thank you," I breathed, hardly daring to believe her words. *Free to go.* I was going to get to walk out of here, back to Sophie, back to my life. I collected my things, slipping my feet into my shoes, relieved to look more like myself once again. And then I strode out into the night, unable to keep myself from smiling. Everything was going to be okay.

Chapter Seven

It was just after 9 p.m. when I finally made it back home. As I got close, I could see people mingling around outside, leaning against the wall, cigarettes glowing brightly in the dark. My throat tightened as I wondered if it was David's family come to confront me, but then I saw the cameras. I paused on the pavement, wondering if I should head straight to Lucas's house, but my hesitation cost me. One of the reporters suddenly looked my way, frowning as he appraised me, and then all at once people were flying into action, shoving their cameras in my face, bombarding me with intrusive questions. *"Isabel, did you know the intruder?" "How do you feel to have been let off?" "Do you think the law is right to allow civilians to kill intruders with no repercussions?" "Did you intend to kill him?"* I wasn't prepared for this onslaught after the horror I'd been through. I knew anything I said would be twisted and shaped to make me the person they wanted to portray. Whether that was the victim or the bad guy, I couldn't yet tell, but I wasn't ready to take the risk that it was the latter.

I kept my chin down, tucked into my chest, my long, tangled hair falling over my face. One of the more daring cameramen squatted on the pavement right in front of me, nearly tripping me over in his determination to get a clear shot of my face. "Excuse me," I muttered, darting round him and rushing up the path. I realised with a wave of relief that they weren't following, instead, they were filming me from the safety of the pavement, unable to cross the invisible barrier onto my property.

The house was dark as I unlocked the door, slipping inside and bolting it shut. I leaned back against the door, scared to move into the thick silence that surrounded me. Despite the knowledge that there were people right outside if I should need their help, being alone in here gave me an uneasy feeling in the pit of my stomach. I was just being silly. I knew David was gone. There would be no corpse waiting for me on the kitchen floor, no threat hiding in the shadows. Yet I had stupidly assumed that I would be given anonymity. Instead, I'd come home to find my privacy in tatters, images of my home being broadcast to the nation. That scared me more than the idea of David's bloody body on my tiles. I took a deep breath, trying to reassure myself that it didn't matter. They were filming in the dark. The location wouldn't be immediately obvious. And in a couple of days this story would blow over and something else would take it's place. I didn't need to work myself into a panic.

Even so, as I walked through the house, I flicked

on every light-switch I passed, breathing easier as the shadows retreated. I forced myself to go straight to the kitchen, refusing to fear what I knew was nothing more than an empty room. On the end of the large central island was a stack of ten and twenty pound notes, along with a few pound coins. There was no sign of the cash box, which I presumed had been claimed as evidence. The tiles, where I'd been sure I'd find a dark stain ready to remind me of what had happened there, were sparkling white, not a mark to be seen. I held my head high as I walked right over the spot where David had fallen, pulling a glass from the cupboard and splashing red wine into it.

I walked around the island to the vintage oak dining table, pulling out a chair and swallowing a big gulp of the wine. I knew this had been the hardest challenge. Coming back to where it had happened, managing not to crumble at the memories of the previous night. So much had changed in the course of twenty-eight hours, it was hard to believe that it hadn't been so much longer. The tiny details flashed on repeat through my mind, David's eyes on mine, the confusion on his face as the knife had pushed through the thin cotton of his t-shirt, then through skin, fat, muscle. The sound as his body had hit the floor. Thud. I couldn't pretend that what I'd done wouldn't impact me for the rest of my life, but I couldn't let it break me either. I was stronger than that.

I reached behind me, grabbing the handset of the house phone from the wall, tangling the curly wire around my fingers as I dialled Lucas's phone number. He answered on the second ring.

"Issy?"

"Yes, it's me."

"Oh, thank god! I was about to come down to the station. What's going on?"

"I'm home. They let me go."

I heard him let out a breath. "It's been all over the news, reporters talking about there being a body, Issy. They've been camped outside your house all day. It's so surreal. What the hell happened?"

Fuck. So they *had* filmed my house in the day. How could they be so irresponsible as to let the world know where to find me? Ignoring the sheen of sweat coating my palms, I told Lucas what I'd told the police. How David had stolen my keys, copied them, come to rob me when he thought I'd be gone, and then attacked me. How I'd had no choice but to stab him in self defence.

"Shit." There was a beat of silence as he absorbed what I'd told him. "I mean... shit, Issy. You must have been terrified."

"I was."

"No wonder you wanted Sophie out in such a hurry."

"Is she okay? I'll come and get her."

"She's fast asleep. And you sound exhausted. Look, why don't you leave her here since she's settled and get some sleep yourself? I'll bring her back first thing."

I hesitated, but only for a moment. I knew she was safe with Lucas. And it wouldn't do for her to see me in such a state, I knew I looked awful. "Okay. Thanks Lucas."

"It's fine. Promise you'll call if you need anything. Even if you just get scared."

"I will. I'm going to run a bath and get an early night. I'll see you in the morning."

"Try and get some sleep."

I hung up and stared into nothingness for a moment, my ears ringing with the silence of the empty house. Logically, I knew I should feel safe now. There had been a threat, I had dealt with it and now everything should return to normal. But I couldn't shake the unease that something was gravely wrong. I reassured myself that I was probably still in shock. Of course I would feel unsettled after what had happened. It would take time to recover from this.

Pouring some more wine into my glass, I checked that the back door was locked, meticulously jiggling all the handles for the windows until I was satisfied that the house was secure. I was just about to climb the stairs when the house phone started ringing, making me jump. I rushed back into the kitchen, grabbing the handset. "Hello?" There was a crackle and then silence. "Hello? Lucas is that you?" There was no answer, and I was just about to hang up when I heard it. Breathing. Slow, deliberate breathing. "Who is this?" I demanded shrilly. "Who – "

The phone clicked as the caller hung up, leaving me feeling shaky and violated. There was something awful about knowing someone could get to you, even in the privacy of your own home. I stood frozen, staring at the phone for a minute, wondering who the caller could have been, my mind taking me to the worst possible places. Then, slowly and carefully I slotted the handset back into it's cradle on the wall. I checked every door and window once more, just to be certain. Moving the curtains in the living room aside ever so slightly, I peeked through the tiny gap and saw that the crowd of journalists had moved off now. I was alone.

What should have been a relief, instead made me feel desperate with the need for them to return, to provide the illusion of safety. They had opened up my life for the world to see and judge and then left me to fend for myself while they went home to their dinner and their safe warm beds. I hoped I wouldn't be the one to pay for their flippancy.

Chapter Eight

I woke with a start as if some distant crash had dragged me to sudden consciousness, my breathing shallow as I strained my ears, sure I would hear the sounds of a window smashing, footsteps creaking up the stairs. Hearing nothing but the gurgle of the water tank, I slipped out of bed, moving to the window, my heart pounding as I tried to catch my breath. I reassured myself that I was safe. It was just a bad dream, nothing more.

Still, I couldn't stop myself from staring outside, shielded from view by the net curtains. Was there someone out there, watching me? An old lady dawdled past, clutching a frayed lead as she walked her Yorkshire terrier towards the green. Ted across the road was washing his car, listening to Bruce

Springsteen as he sploshed soapy water over the shining bonnet. The world looked utterly ordinary. Glancing at the clock, I was startled to see it was almost 9 a.m. Lucas should have arrived with Sophie by now. Why hadn't he come? Had something happened?

I felt shaken. The stabbing, the arrest and then to top it all off, that prank phone call. It was all too much. Despite feeling like I might collapse from exhaustion, I'd been so worked up I couldn't settle to sleep last night, my mind racing as I'd tried to work out who it could have been. Was someone playing games with me, or was it something more sinister? I'd killed a man. You couldn't walk away from that without some repercussions. People would be angry. Was this the start of them punishing me?

I had to stay calm. One prank call was not enough to get worked up over. I was being ridiculous. Paranoid. I forced down the fear that was trying to bubble up like molten lava, and made myself go through my normal morning rituals, showering, dressing, putting on make-up and a pair of heels.

By the time I made it downstairs I felt strong again. Braver. The kettle was just coming to the boil when the doorbell rang, accompanied by enthusiastic banging and squeals of delight. *Finally!* Flinging the door open, I swooped Sophie into my arms, hugging her tightly. "Hi baby, I missed you." I let myself pause to inhale the sweet smell of her head, feeling the reassuring weight of her as she leaned against me.

"I missed you too, Mummy," she said, wriggling out of my grasp to look up at me. "Did you finish your police lady job now?"

"I think it's finished, sweetie, but we'll have to wait and see if they need me again."

She gave a dramatic sigh. "Okay. But next time you should come home in time for my bedtime. Oscar snores!"

"I do not!" he said, folding his arms crossly.

"You do. And you have wind!"

"Well, that bit's true I suppose," he admitted, with a proud grin.

"Can Oscar come and play in my room, Mummy? Sophie asked, bouncing on her tiptoes.

I nodded. "But not for long. We're off to visit Auntie Bonnie in a little while."

"Okay. Come on Oscar." They giggled and ran towards the stairs, already focused on some imaginary world they'd created.

Lucas stepped forward, closing the front door behind him. Wordlessly, he wrapped his arms around me, and I felt grateful for the brief moment of security. "Have you looked out there?" he asked, stepping back.

"Earlier. Why?"

He shook his head. "Just the vultures circling for scraps again."

"They're back? They didn't film the kids?"

"I put my hands in front of the camera. I don't think they got a clear shot, but they bloody tried."

My heart was pounding, my hands forming into fists. "Don't they know they have no right to do this! Sophie is an at risk child. I should go out there and – "

"Don't. That's exactly what they want, to provoke you into reacting. They want something interesting to hand into their bosses, they don't give a damn about how that affects you. You know that, Issy. Take a breath and let it go. They'll be gone soon enough."

I nodded stiffly, knowing he was right yet hating it all the same. I unfurled my fingers, inhaling a deep breath into my lungs, feeling some of the anger leave my tense body.

"How are you doing?" he asked softly.

"Oh, I'm fine."

"Issy."

"Really Lucas, I'm okay. Just a bit shaken, that's all. And fed up with being treated like public property. I just want everything to go back to normal." Lucas rubbed his palm across the thick black stubble that coated his chin, frowning. For a man as tall and strong as he was, he was surprisingly transparent when it came to wearing his state of mind on his sleeve. He could never hide how he'd been feeling, and his crumpled shirt and unshaven face showed me more than his words ever could. I knew he somehow felt responsible for me and my twin, Bonnie. Our father had died when we were barely more than toddlers and our mother had committed suicide when we were teens as a result of bipolar disorder. After we'd been orphaned, our big sister Roxy had been the person we had both turned to for comfort and security. When she'd died from a brain tumour leaving Lucas alone to care for baby Oscar, Bonnie and I had been left without a trace of family, save for a widowed brother-in-law and our baby nephew.

Lucas could have easily cut us out, walked away, started something new with someone else. He could have hated the reminder we gave him of the life that had once been his. But he hadn't. He'd stuck by both of us, supported us emotionally and stopped me from falling apart on more than one occasion. Bonnie had spiralled into her own battle with bipolar, lashing out, disappearing for months at a time, and returning no better.

In the six years since Roxy had died, Bonnie had been living the same endless cycle. She would go through weeks of mania before sinking into the deepest depression I had ever known her to experience, eventually landing herself back in hospital. It was draining to stand by as a helpless witness with no way of reaching her. After a while, I had begun to realise that she didn't *want* to get better. Whereas our mother had truly believed she didn't need her pills, wasn't sick at all, Bonnie knew what she was doing. She chose to give into her mental illness as an escape. She couldn't bear to live in the raw truth of her reality.

Inevitably, she would be discharged after putting on a good enough show for the overworked doctors to believe she was going to stick to the plan, take her meds, come to her appointments this time, but it never lasted. She didn't want it, and as much as I had tried over the years, I had finally realised, you can't make anyone do anything if they really don't want to. Bonnie was currently sectioned under the mental health act, safe in hospital, and though I hated her having to be there, the truth was it was the only time I could breath easy knowing she wasn't out harming herself.

Lucas raised an eyebrow at me, clearly not ready to drop his interrogations. I turned away, walking briskly into the kitchen, leaving him to follow behind as I spooned instant coffee into mugs, avoiding his probing eyes. "Isabel. You killed someone."

I froze, my hands gripping the jar of coffee, the hairs raising on my arms as he spoke the words without any effort to filter them. "I know, Lucas," I said, my voice barely a whisper. "I know I did. What else could I do? It was him or me, and Sophie was upstairs alone. What would you have done, Lucas?" I pinched the bridge of my nose between my fingers, the beginnings of a headache spreading across my temples.

"I'm not trying to put blame on you, Issy. Not at all. But you can't just go through something like that and then say you're fine. You don't have to be fine."

"Yes, I do. I won't let him win, Lucas. I won't let him affect me. I have responsibilities, people who rely on me – Sophie, my colleagues... I don't have the luxury of falling to pieces now. So yes, I killed a man, and I'm fine." I slammed down a cup of strong coffee on the breakfast bar in front of him. "And I'd prefer not to discuss it anymore, actually." I glared at him, challenging him to push me.

He held up his hands in mock surrender. "Fine. We'll drop it. But if you change your mind and need someone to talk to – "

"I'll know where to find you." I leaned over the counter, squeezing his bear-like hand briefly. "Thank you," I added softly.

"Anytime. You know that."

"I do." I checked my watch. "I need to get going in a minute. Bonnie will be waiting."

He nodded. "I would offer to join you, but I promised Oscar I'd take him ice-skating. We missed it Monday night. I had to work late."

"Everything okay?"

"Yep. Just a labradoodle needing an emergency C-Section. Four very sweet, healthy pups. And Oscar forgave me when he got to come and see them. But I promised we'd go today."

"That's fine, I'll tell her you said hi shall I?" I offered, secretly relieved that he wouldn't be joining me. I had no intention of telling Bonnie what I'd been up to this past few days. In fact, Lucas and I would have to have a chat about that in the near future. I couldn't risk her ever finding out about what I'd done. It would destroy her.

Chapter Nine

There was a time when Bonnie and I had looked so utterly identical that sometimes even our mother couldn't tell us apart. As children it had been an endless source of amusement, tricking our friends, switching places, confusing people. We'd drawn comfort in knowing that we weren't alone in the world. We were two peas in a pod and we would always have that.

People said we were beautiful, with our soft green eyes and flowing ginger curls that ended at the base of our spines. We'd always been slender, athletic, but never thin, and whenever someone offered us a compliment I'd always been proud of my sister rather than consider that I was included in the kindness. Though we looked the same, our personalities could not have been more different. Bonnie was confident, outspoken and full of adventure. She wanted to try everything, see everything and she never turned down a new experience. I was the complete opposite. I liked time to be alone, to sit quietly in my own thoughts. I liked to analyse things, observe from a distance, but never be the centre of attention. Despite our outward similarities, I had always believed that Bonnie was the more beautiful of the two of us. Her confidence made her radiant. Every time she suffered a trauma, rather than wilting, she would defiantly hold up her head and let it wash over her like nothing mattered. Like nothing could dent her. But I knew the truth.

These days, there was no chance of anyone mixing us up. Even a complete stranger would have no difficulty in telling us apart. Over the past seven years, Bonnie had lost so much weight that at her worst she'd been nothing more than a walking skeleton. Two years ago, she had hacked off all of her hair in a fit of rage. I would never be able to erase the image of that moment from my mind – walking in to find her sitting on the end of the bed, those shining silver scissors open on the carpet by her feet, the deep red welts that formed as she clawed at her skin. Seeing the look of absolute anguish written on her sunken features, the tufts of copper hair sticking out in random clumps, contrasting vividly with her ghost white face, her angular cheek bones. She'd looked like a fragile baby bird fallen from the nest.

Now, two years later, she'd gained a little weight back, making her merely skinny rather than skeletal, and her hair had grown into a chunky shoulder length bob, serving as a reminder of that awful night. She was sitting by the large bay window in the communal living area as Sophie and I approached, her gaze travelling far off across the garden. She wore a long fleece dressing gown, concealing her arms and chest, but just a peek beneath the thick fabric would reveal the story of her roller-coaster journey with mental health. Bright sleeves of tattoos were now ridged and distorted, a consequence of the blades she'd dragged repeatedly over her skin. Scars mingled with skulls, though from a distance she still looked like a work of art. Beautiful, but broken.

"Auntie Bonnie!" Sophie squealed as she spotted her. Bonnie turned, a wide smile on her face as Sophie leaped into her lap, wrapping her arms tightly around her neck. Bonnie kissed her all over her face, her eyes sparking. She looked well, but I was too jaded to get excited about it. I'd been pulled into that trap before.

"Hey, Sis," she said, looking up from beneath the thick blanket of Sophie's long dark hair. She positioned her on one thigh and pulled a stray brunette hair from her mouth. "Bleaugh!"

Sophie giggled and I leaned down to kiss Bonnie on the cheek. "Sorry we're late. Lucas popped by." I dropped my bag on the floor and slumped into the high-backed armchair opposite her.

"That's okay. I only just got out of a review with my doctor anyway."

"Yeah?"

She nodded. "It went well." She grinned mischievously. "I'm going to be out in a week!"

I felt like someone had dumped a sack of rocks in my belly. The cold, hard, heavy pain in my gut quickly spread across my chest. My throat was tight as I tried to speak. "So soon? That can't be right. Are you sure that's what he said, Bon?"

"It's been seven weeks. And I'm better now. I *am,*" she insisted, seeing the incredulous expression I had pulled. "I'm sick of being locked up here. I want to be free."

"But..." I couldn't think what to say. She *couldn't* come home, not while I was in the middle of a media scandal. Not when I didn't know if I could protect her. Sophie was watching me, her eyes alert as she listened to my every word. "Hey, Sophie, look!" I pointed out to the garden where a group of children were throwing water balloons filled with brightly coloured paint at a huge canvas laid out on the grass. "That looks like fun. Why don't you go and join in while I have a chat with your Auntie Bonnie?" She nodded, bounding off of Bonnie's lap and sprinting out the side door. We watched her little dark head as she sprinted across the garden to where the two play specialists were putting on the activity for visiting children.

"Bonnie," I said, taking her hand in mine. "I know you're bored in here, sweetheart. I don't blame you for wanting to get out sooner rather than later.

But you can't rush these things. You *know* that. Remember last time?"

"This time it's different."

"How? How can it be? You'll come out with all the right intentions, but we both know that in a fortnight, you'll have flushed your pills. You need to stay here for longer, much longer. You need to have the support of the people in here to help you, to make taking your pills into a habit. It's too hard when you're out on your own and expected to look after yourself. The temptation to let go will always be there, Bon. You need to make sure you're strong enough to not give into it. And I don't think you're there yet."

"I agree," she said, sitting back with a smug grin on her face.

"You do? So you'll stay here?"

"Nope."

"What?"

"I don't need to. You and I both know I won't take my pills. The docs know that too. So they've given me a depo injection instead. Right in the arse cheek! Bloody hurt actually, but they said it'll last four weeks. I just have to commit to coming back to top it up once a month. I can do that, Issy. It's not something I have to think about every single day. I can do it."

"Can you?" I asked uncertainly.

"Yes. The drugs are already in my system now, and as long as I'm thinking straight, I won't have any reason not to come back."

"But if you miss the appointment... if you forget... or..."

"Or decide I don't want this?"

I nodded. She leaned forward, taking my hand and looking me in the eye. There was always so much intensity in her eyes, so many secrets and stories just beneath the surface. She had a way of making you feel like you were the only person in the room, that she was sharing her soul with you. Sometimes she was. But other times, she was simply trying her best to manipulate you. To make you feel so warm and special that you couldn't even think of arguing with her. Right now, I couldn't tell which one this was. "Look, Issy," she said in her husky tones. "I know I've given you no reason to trust me. But you've got to believe that this time I *want* to get better. When I came in this Summer, I was so close to just giving up. I could see myself doing what mum did – "

"Bonnie!"

"No need to act surprised. You know as well as I do that I was heading down that path. And I wanted to. If I hadn't been sectioned, I would be dead now. No doubt. But I'm not. And all this time in here, thinking about how close I came to ending everything... It makes you think." She gave a shrug and sat back in her chair, still staring at me. "I want to live. I want to see Oscar and Sophie grow up. I want to do something other than sit around here waiting for my meals to come and doing shitty watercolour paintings. I'm missing so much. I have already missed so much, thrown away years of my life that I'll never get back. I don't want to keep doing this same shit over and over again. So yes, I can do it. And I will."

I'd never heard her speak with such conviction about getting well before. She meant it. Whether she could do it or not was still up for debate, but I could see that she meant to try. She wasn't putting on an act. But one determined speech of intent couldn't undo the past seven years. I couldn't ignore everything we'd been through, the times she'd gone walkabout, the rages and the parties and the pain she'd inflicted on herself and everyone around her. I couldn't see her go through all of that again. I wouldn't put Sophie through it. And selfishly, I couldn't deal with her being out right now. I was struggling as it was without adding extra responsibility into the mix. I leaned back in my chair, wishing I could go back to bed and hide under the covers.

"Are you okay?" she asked, frowning. "You don't look yourself."

I wasn't myself. The truth was I had no idea who I was now. But I wasn't about to tell her that. "I'm fine," I told her with a tight smile. Sophie's small fist knocked on the window, and she beckoned for us to come outside with her, saving me from having to talk any more. "Come on," I said, grabbing my bag as I waved to Sophie. "Let's get some fresh air."

Chapter Ten

I loved the peace and quiet of the early morning. It was something I'd appreciated so much more since becoming a parent. Time to wake up slowly, adjust to the rhythm of the day before the rush of questions and conversation began. Sophie was still fast asleep having stayed up late to watch Aladdin in my bed last night, but it was the first day of half term and we had hours until we had to go anywhere. I loved our little sleepover parties, just the two of us. We'd snuggled up with a bowl of toffee popcorn, and I'd plaited her hair as she dozed in my lap.

I smiled at the memory, dropping my teacup into the sink and turning on the small TV on the kitchen wall. A tiny gasp escaped my lips as I was brought face to face with an image of David Harrison taking up half the screen. The newsreader was talking to some expert as she grilled him on the law on defending yourself in your own home. I was relieved to hear that he seemed to be on my side.

"If you're going to go uninvited into a person's property, you have to understand the risk you're taking," he said, his glasses glinting in the studio lights.

"Shouldn't Isabel Cormack face charges though? Isn't killing him an extreme reaction?"

"Simply put, no. None of us know how we would react if faced with an intruder in our home. The police have told us that Miss Cormack asked Mr Harrison to leave her property, at which point he came at her with a weapon – "

"A screwdriver."

"Yes. Which can easily become a weapon in the wrong hands. As I said, she had every right to defend herself in her own home. Not to mention the fact that there was a six year old child upstairs. The fault was with David Harrison, and he paid the price for his reckless actions."

I sat down, unable to gather the willpower to turn off the TV. The newsreader turned back to the camera and introduced a reporter on location, and the picture of David mercifully disappeared. The camera panned out and there on the street beside the reporter was a man who made my blood run cold. I stood up, walking to the television, shocked at what I was seeing. That was him! That was David! The reporter began to speak. "I have Lee Harrison here with me, David's twin brother."

He had a twin? I'd killed his twin! My thoughts flew to Bonnie and how I would feel if someone took her from me. I would want to murder them. I could see from Lee's eyes that he was no different.

"How do you feel about the law in this situation, Mr Harrison?" the reporter asked. "Do you agree with the decision to let Miss Cormack go without charge?" He stepped closer to him, his microphone outstretched.

Lee's lip was shaking as he stared into the camera, hatred pouring from him as though he were looking right through the screen, into my soul. "She *murdered* my brother. David would *never* have broken in and attacked her. *Never*. He didn't have a violent bone in his body. That woman killed my brother, and she will pay for what she did. I'll make sure of that."

The screen went black as I hit the power switch, the image of those hate filled eyes, *David's eyes*, burned into my mind. He wanted justice. Or was it revenge he craved? My breathing was shallow, my fingernails tearing jagged cuts through my already damaged palms. I prised my hands open, laying them flat against the cool worktop. I sucked in several deep breaths, silently counting to ten. Then,

I plastered a smile on my face and went to wake Sophie.

The air was noticeably cooler than it had been in the past few weeks. The summer had stretched on longer than usual, well into late October, but though the sky was clear and blue, there was a feeling of Autumn in the air now. The leaves were turning golden and dropping in haphazard patterns on the ground, and I made a vow to enjoy what was left of the sunny days before they were gone completely. The tinny carnival music was blaring as we walked across the field towards the big top tent, Sophie skipping along beside me, her small hand squeezing mine. Her excitement was palpable and I couldn't help but smile as I watched her. Out here in the bright sunshine, surrounded by happy, laughing families, it was hard to feel scared. Lee was angry and grieving and looking for someone to blame, and of course I would be the person he focused on. But he'd publicly declared his intent to make me pay for David's death. If anything were to happen to me now, he would be the chief suspect. I was sure that he was already regretting those hasty words said in anger, he couldn't really mean them.

Sophie pulled at my hand as she led me through the wide entrance into the darkness of the circus tent. It was stuffy, loud and crowded, the type of place I would have avidly avoided before Sophie came into my life, but sacrificing my eardrums and comfort was a small price to pay for her happiness. We joined the queue of excited groups waiting to be shown to their seats and I felt the heel of my stiletto sink into the soft mud.

"Isabel Cormack!" came a voice from behind me. I yanked my heel free, turning around to see who'd called me.

"Oh, hi Claire," I called. The tiny statured, big

bosomed woman muscled her way through the crowd towards me, a wide smile on her warm, face.

"Long time no see!" she said, her rosy cheeks rounder than ever as she leaned in to give me a hug. She pushed her glasses up her nose, and I was reminded of the many hours we'd spent working together before I'd finally given into the pressure from my superiors and accepted a promotion. Claire and I had both qualified as social workers the same year, and together we'd seen things that still to this day gave me nightmares. We had spent numerous nights sobbing together over a bottle of wine as we asked each other how people could treat their children so horrifically. "So how's the new job working out?" she asked. I let myself breathe a tiny sigh of relief, realising that she obviously hadn't been watching the news over the weekend.

"It's good," I smiled. Sophie moulded herself to my leg and I put my arm around her. "The term-time only hours are a big bonus. I get to be with Sophie for all the school holidays."

Claire nodded. "I had to book the day off. But Morgan was desperate for me to bring him – he's just in the loo with his Dad." She tilted her head to one side, twisting her mouth into a curious smile. "So, you really don't miss the action? I never thought you'd accept the office job, you always loved being right in the thick of it. I've never known anyone as passionate about helping children as you, Isabel. You surprised everyone when you gave it up to do the behind the scenes stuff."

"I know." She was right. I had thrown myself so deeply into my cases, it was as if every child I worked with became a part of my soul. I loved being able to walk into their pitiful excuse for a home and take them away from the pain they'd been forced to endure. I loved that because of what I did, their lives were made better.

Sophie had been the last child I'd ever been assigned to investigate. After her headteacher had reported frequent absences and unexplained bruising, I'd been sent to her house where I'd found her father drunk and belligerent. Her mother had been passed out in the living room, a needle still wedged in the crook of her arm. I'd left the police constable who'd accompanied me to deal with the parents, and made my way slowly upstairs. When I'd pushed open the door, Sophie's big brown eyes had shone out of the darkness, the hope in them engulfing me in a wave of protective love I'd never known the strength of. Her tiny wrist was bound to her bed frame, her body half starved, her lips dry and cracked from dehydration. Her room had been absolutely bare, save for the metal bed-frame and the stained, unmade mattress.

We later discovered that her entire body was black and blue from years of physical abuse, and she had an untreated fracture in her forearm. She'd been living with monsters. Monsters who were now, thankfully, behind bars. I had crossed the room moving slowly towards her, speaking soft words of reassurance, so aware of how terrified she must be. I'd untied her bonds, expecting her to dive away from me, cower in the corner of the room, but instead, she'd thrown herself into my arms, whispering in my ear, "I wished for you, I wished you would come for me." I'd known then that this wasn't just another case. From that moment onwards, my whole life became about one thing. Adopting Sophie. Giving her the life she deserved.

It had taken months to get her out of foster care. I'd spent my nights filling out paperwork, going over every single document to make sure I'd not missed anything out. And finally, to the shock of my colleagues, I gave into my bosses and accepted the promotion they'd been pushing me to take for so long. I didn't need to be out in the field now. I would channel all my energy into helping Sophie heal from what she'd lived through. The new position had come with a massive pay rise and child friendly hours. I didn't regret it at all.

"No, I don't miss it," I smiled. "I was ready for a change. It was time."

Claire grinned. "I can understand that. It suits you." I raised an eyebrow. "Motherhood, I mean."

"Mummy," Sophie whispered. She pointed at the usher who was waiting for us to follow him.

"I have to go, it was lovely to see you, Claire."

"Same. We should catch up over coffee soon. I bet Sophie and Morgan would get on well."

"Yes, let's." I blew her a kiss and rushed after the usher, settling Sophie down in the seat beside me. A few minutes later a clown cycled out onto the circular stage on a bright green unicycle, a water-pistol grasped in his hands. Sophie squealed in delight as a blast of cool water hit us, her smile unbroken as the water trickled from her eyebrows, down her cheeks.

The clown looped his way around the stage, then artfully crashed into a post. Clumsily, he pulled himself up to his feet, only to slip in a pool of water again, landing heavily on his back. Sophie was breathless with laughter, the joyful sound rumbling from deep within her belly, her peals of giggles absolutely contagious.

I watched her face as she focused intently on the show, fascinated by the effect it was having on her. A shiver built in me and I got the sudden feeling I was being watched, the back of my neck prickling uncomfortably. I turned in my seat, scanning the faces in the crowd, expecting to see someone staring at me, but there were only smiling children and parents on a family day out. I shook my head, turning back to the stage, but I couldn't shake the feeling. Someone was behind me, watching me. I was certain of it.

Chapter Eleven

I couldn't relax. I hadn't actually seen anyone watching me, but determined as I was to enjoy the day with Sophie, something felt off. I couldn't stop fidgeting, my eyes darting around the dark tent, straining to see the people standing in the shadowy corners. When the show ended, I leapt up relieved to finally get out into the open.

I lifted Sophie into my arms, carrying her through the crowd. Breaking into the cool fresh air I placed her on the grass, breathing heavily as I scanned the people filtering from the big top. Not a single person was looking at me. Everyone was wrapped up in their own lives, they didn't care who I was or what I was doing. I was being stupid, paranoid.

We'd come to a stop beside a row of stalls selling flashing light up toys, candyfloss and sweets. Sophie's eyes were trained on her feet and my stomach lurched in an uncomfortable mixture of sadness and anger for the way she'd been treated by the people who should have protected her. Even now, she could never bring herself to ask for extra. All the other girls and boys were whining as they negotiated a lollypop, expertly guiding their parents and grandparents to the back of the queue, but not Sophie. She'd been conditioned to believe that she didn't deserve nice things, treats, *love* even, and I was determined to break that belief and show her otherwise.

I took her small hand in my own and we joined the queue for the nearest stall. "What would you like, darling? You can choose anything." She simply shook her head, blushing to the roots of her hair. I looked up at the colourful stall, trying to think of what she might like – what I might have liked as a little girl.

"What can I get you, love?" the woman asked.

"I'll take that flashing star wand, please. And one of those enormous dummy lollies, I think." Sophie's hand tightened around mine and I hid a smile, knowing I'd made the right choice. I handed the wand to her and looped the ribbon of the lolly around her neck. She looked like she might actually burst with gratitude.

"Thank you so much, Mummy, I love you," she said softly, her hands wrapping around the wand until her knuckles turned white.

"It's yours to keep. I love you too, sweetie, so much." I took one of her small hands in mine and we began the walk back home. Crossing the road away from the hubbub of the field, we walked in silence, taking the quiet back-roads to avoid the crowds. Families were drifting back to cars or laughing in groups as they walked back to their own homes.

We turned onto a long residential road and I glanced over my shoulder, feeling suddenly exposed. A little way behind me was a man, his baseball cap pulled low over his face, shielding his features from view, his hands hidden in the deep pockets of a thick bomber jacket. He was tall, with broad shoulders, and I wouldn't have looked twice at him if it weren't for the fact that when I glanced behind me, he froze. It was only for a fragment of a second, so fleeting it could have been ignored, but I knew I'd seen it, and suddenly I was sure that he wasn't just an innocent pedestrian. He was following me.

My whole body instantly went into overdrive, the instinct to pick Sophie up and run flat out until we reached our house pulsing through me, the panic at what this man could want, who he could be, making my heart pound. But there was nowhere to run. I was wearing three inch heels, and Sophie, light as she may be, was still six years old. The street was long and straight, with no side roads to cut through, and I knew that if he gave chase, he'd catch us in seconds. There were numerous vans parked along the curb, all now potential dangers, traps with people lurking inside them, ready to grab the pair of us and take us who knows where.

Instead of giving into the urge to run, I settled for speeding up my walking pace, swinging Sophie's hand playfully, singing loudly to diffuse my nerves. The road seemed to go on forever, but though a man with legs as long as his could have easily overtaken us, I could still hear his footsteps twenty paces back. He never got closer. I kept hoping he'd turn into a gate, disappear inside one of the houses, but he never did.

We finally rounded the corner, and I chanced

another look over my shoulder as we crossed the road. There was no sign of him. We reached the end of our street and I saw him come round the corner, hesitate for a second and then follow in the exact path we'd taken. We were close to home now. Close enough that we might just make it. "Hey, Sophie, want to show me your fastest run? I bet I can beat you home!"

"You know I can run faster than you," she giggled.

"Show me."

She took off like a racing dog, bolting along the pavement with incredible speed. I had never been able to keep up with her when it came to races, but this time I didn't have the luxury of power-walking along in her wake. I heard footsteps speeding up behind me and broke into a sprint. My stiletto slipped on an uneven strip of pavement, my ankle twisting painfully, but I couldn't stop. I gritted my teeth, continuing on, feeling the unwavering stare of the man behind me. Sophie reached our driveway before me and I was relieved to see that the reporters weren't there this time. Yanking my keys from my bag without slowing, I pelted up the drive, rammed them in the lock and swung Sophie inside, slamming the door behind me and bolting it shut. "You won!" I sang, hugging her tightly, my arms shaking violently from fear and exertion.

"Told you I'm fast," she grinned.

"You are!" I strode past her into the living room, moving straight to the window. My breath caught as I looked outside. There at the end of the driveway was the man who'd followed us home. I hadn't imagined it. *I knew it!* He was standing facing the house, his cap pulled low.

Who the hell was he? A reporter? One of David's relatives trying to get back at me? I couldn't see his face, it could have been his brother, Lee who'd threatened me on the news this morning. It had to be him. A wave of fury washed over me. How dare he victimise me, stalk me and my child when I'd done nothing but defend my family. How dare he come to my home! I wasn't going to let him frighten me. *Fuck him!*

"Sophie, take your wand upstairs and play for a little while so I can sort dinner, okay?"

"Yes, Mummy." I walked her out to the hallway and she clattered up the stairs. I waited until I heard her door click shut, then I turned, sliding open the bolts on the front door. Yanking it wide, I stormed out onto the driveway, ready to face whoever it was, my heart pounding against my ribcage, only to find the street deserted.

He had gone.

Chapter Twelve

The phone had rung just as I was putting Sophie to bed. I'd let it go unanswered, closing her bedroom door to muffle the sound and reading her story in a cheery voice. After she'd fallen asleep, I'd crept downstairs and picked it up, dialling 1471 to check the number. It was withheld, of course. Half an hour later it had sounded again, and despite myself, I hadn't been able to resist picking it up. The sound of heavy breathing had filled my ears, and this time I'd been the first to slam down the handset. I'd considered unplugging it entirely, but then, responsibility had kicked in. What if Lucas had an emergency and my mobile didn't have a signal? What if the hospital called about Bonnie?

I'd crept into Sophie's bed, needing to be close to

her, to protect her from unseen dangers, listening to every creak and gurgle the house made and getting no sleep at all. I'd padded out of her room before she woke, coming downstairs to make coffee as a new day dawned. The exhaustion was beginning to make me feel ill. Since David's death, I'd managed no more than a few hours of sleep most nights, and I felt sick and dizzy all the time. A never ending stream of *what ifs* ran through my head, and every time I closed my eyes, I replayed the events of that day. I couldn't stop thinking about what might have happened if things had gone differently. Reliving the horror of what I'd been forced to do.

As I stumbled down the stairs, my bleary eyes were drawn to the blood red envelope sitting on the mat by the front door. I froze, my foot hovering inches above the bottom step, my body refusing to move forward. It hadn't been there last night, and it was far too early for the postman to have been. This had been delivered by hand in the dead of night. Someone had tiptoed up the path while I'd lain wide awake and crippled with fear beside my sleeping daughter. They'd been so close to us, one inch of wooden door separating us, providing the false illusion of safety.

I hated feeling vulnerable, powerless. I'd worked so hard to break those habits, to be strong and brave. I was disgusted to realise quite how much I was being affected by everything that was going on. I ran my fingernails back and forth across my lower lip, pushing into the soft, chapped skin, studying the envelope from afar. Then I sucked in a breath and propelled myself forward, crouching down to pick it up. There was no name on the thick claret paper, no address. I ripped it open, pulling out a plain white card and opening it without ceremony.

The message was short and to the point, but it was enough to make me feel like I might actually collapse. I didn't. Instead I read the words again, trying to work out if I recognised the blocky handwriting.

Now I know where you live.

It had to be the person who'd followed us home yesterday. Of course it had been a stupid idea to lead him right to our house, but what other choice did I have? The nearest cafe was ten minutes in the opposite direction, and I had been too scared to add any extra time to our journey, so sure that any minute he would break into a run and tackle me to the pavement. I'd needed the safety of familiar ground and a locked door, but now he knew exactly where to find me. Was it Lee? Did he really hate me so much that he would try to scare a single mother for defending herself in her own home? Or was the letter from someone else who'd been trying to track me down? I shuddered at the thought, my insides turning to ice at the merest hint of the possibility.

I'd known I was vulnerable the moment I'd seen the reporters outside my house. I'd known I could be in a lot of danger. If only I knew for certain that it was Lee, then I could deal with it. The not knowing was causing me almost as much stress as the calls, the stalking. If I knew who it was, I could search them out, get the upper hand and confront them.

I wondered whether I should call the police, let them know I was being harassed. If they'd even care? There could be fingerprints on the letterbox? Or maybe they could trace the calls somehow? I dismissed the idea almost as soon as it popped into my head. I didn't want to speak to them again. I wanted to be out of their thoughts for good. But there *was* one person I could call.

I pushed the card back into it's envelope and

placed it onto the top shelf of the kitchen cupboard where Sophie wouldn't find it, then I made a strong cup of coffee and sat down at the table. I took a sip, wincing as the bitter liquid burned my tongue, but feeling myself breath easier as the caffeine travelled through my bloodstream. Then I picked up the phone and called Lucas.

The long chat with my brother-in-law had helped. As had the three cups of filter coffee I'd drunk. I'd told Lucas a watered down version of what had been happening, the prank calls, the man who'd followed me home, but not everything. Not the fears I wasn't ready to put words to. Lucas had been exactly what I needed. He was good at listening. His deep, strong voice made me feel safe. He'd told me I was to call him if I ever felt scared, and I'd promised I would. Just knowing he was there was enough.

Sophie was making mud pies in the garden, digging ferociously, covering her waterproof dungarees in dirt and slop as she mixed water from her watering can into the bowl, breaking up leaves and sprinkling them in too, for added flavour apparently. I was watching her through the window as I ate a sliced apple, feeling so much more relaxed than I had earlier, when the phone rang. My stomach flipped, my appetite leaving me instantly. I pushed the plate of fruit away and reached over, lifting the phone to my ear.

"Yes?"

"Isabel Cormack?"

"Yes, who's this?"

"This is PC Raynar, down at St Aldates station. Are you okay to talk for a minute?"

I felt as if my heart had turned to rock in my chest, my mind flashing from one thought to the next without pausing to rest. What did she want?

They had released me, I was free, they said it was over. Would they come back for me now? Take me away? Take Sophie? I felt the beginnings of a panic attack working its way through my body and coughed, trying to catch my breath, to release the pressure settling heavily over my lungs. "Excuse me," I managed to splutter. "I was just finishing lunch. I think a bit of food went down the wrong way."

"Are you okay now?" came the woman's voice.

"Yes, of course. I'm fine. How can I help you?" I glanced out to the garden, wondering if we would have time to run if they said they were coming for me, then shook my head. That was a ridiculous idea.

"Actually, it's more an offer to help you," she continued.

"What do you mean?"

"It's standard procedure to contact the victims after incidents such as the one you were... involved in."

Victim. She had referred to me as the victim. That had to be a good sign, didn't it? I felt some of the tension leave my shoulders, but didn't release my tight grip on the phone.

"Right. Okay."

"We just wanted to check how you were doing, and ask if you'd like a referral to speak to a therapist?"

"A therapist?"

"Yes, it's quite normal to have a lot of intense emotions and fears after something like this. Often people find it helpful to talk it through with someone qualified to deal with post traumatic stress and other issues."

"No, I don't want to talk to anyone."

"Are you sure? It's completely confidential."

"I'm quite sure. Thank you."

There was a short pause. "Okay. If you change

your mind, just call the station and we'll have someone arrange it for you."

"I won't change my mind. But thank you for your time."

I hung up the phone with a juddering breath, grasping the edge of the table for support. Therapy? Bloody therapy! Oh, if only she knew what a can of worms that would be opening up. No, I wouldn't be going down that route. I had too many secrets that needed to stay locked up to ever have the luxury of letting go on some squashy sofa with a sympathetic (to begin with) and later disgusted and horrified therapist, listening to me slice open my mind and lay it out before her. Absolutely not.

Chapter Thirteen

Half term had flown by in a blur of park visits, picnics in the garden, Lego building and making dens out of the furniture. I'd tried to keep busy, more so than usual even, desperate to keep my mind on Sophie and ignore the lingering threat of being followed. Lucas and Oscar had been round twice and hearing him refer to "The Stalker" in his jokey light-hearted voice had taken the edge off my fear somewhat. It was hard to be scared with Lucas around. The calls had continued though, almost always in the evenings when nobody else was around. It was as if the caller knew, as if they were watching the comings and goings of the house. I had run to the front door flinging it open and glaring out at the world on several occasions, sure that I'd see someone lurking with a mobile phone in hand, enjoying the thrill of torturing me, but though the hairs had raised on the back of my neck, I'd never actually seen anyone there.

To add to the stress of the calls, I'd been sure we were being followed on a further two occasions after the circus incident. I'd learned my lesson though, always sticking to the busy main roads or driving if we had to go anywhere we might be exposed to danger. I'd cancelled plans a couple of times when I just couldn't face going out.

It was almost a relief to take Sophie back to school now that the half-term holiday had come to an end. The constant vigilance combined with putting on a positive front was draining, and I was glad that soon I would be able to look over my shoulder without causing her to panic. I was desperate to get back to the office too, to surround myself with activity and people, but annoyingly, I had two days of working from home to endure first while the office was being re-painted.

Sophie was dressed in her red mac and yellow boots, her long dark hair plaited over her shoulder as she kicked and splashed her way through the deep puddles lining the pavement. She looked like a doll, so perfect it was hard to believe she was even real.

"Mummy, if a butterfly gets back inside its cuckoo, uh?"

"Cocoon?"

"Yes, that. If he crawls back inside it and goes to sleep for a really long time, can he turn himself back into a caterpillar if he wants to?"

I shook my head. "No, he can't. Once you've been through a transformation that huge, there's no going back. You're changed forever."

She considered this for a moment, kicking her boots through the puddles. "You have to be really sure you want to be a butterfly then. If you have to stay that way forever."

"That's true. There's lots of good things about being a butterfly though. They get to fly."

"Yes."

I smiled down at her. "Would you rather be a butterfly or a caterpillar?"

She screwed up her face. "I think I'd choose butterfly. But there's lots of cool things about being a caterpillar too. I like the way they bunch up their bodies when they move. It's like they're really concentrating on getting somewhere."

I laughed. "I agree. Caterpillars are pretty cool too." We turned into the gates for her school and Sophie spotted her best friend Joanna, running off to play before the bell rang. In a tight circle near the main door stood four women, dressed just like me. High heels, expensive clothes, designer handbags. I paused for a second, seeing Megan glance my way then quickly avert her eyes. So, they'd seen the news. Of course they had. The story would have been all over Facebook and Twitter and these women made it their business to know all the hottest gossip.

These were the people I called my friends. Women who would have been the popular girls in school, who wouldn't have given someone like me a second thought. They were callous, shallow and could cut you out in the blink of an eye if you didn't meet their high standards. I'd seen it done plenty of times before, to women who wore the wrong shoes or had chipped nail varnish at parents evening. Fair-weather friends, but I knew that already. I had chosen them for their inability to look beneath the surface. And much as I hated it, I needed them for my place in society. To complete the picture of who I was. Popular. Accepted. Adored. Envied.

And now, I was faced with a situation that could

go two ways. Become an object of pity and gossip, ostracised and out in the cold. Or, win them over with the only thing they could understand. I knew what I had to do. I ran my hand through my wavy hair, making sure it was perfect, then swallowed my pride.

"Ladies! You will not believe the gossip I have!" I called, walking into their circle with my head held high, no trace of insecurity or shame to be seen. They paused, shocked. I hadn't taken the expected action and slumped off with my tail between my legs.

There was an exchange of uneasy glances between the four of them and then unable to resist, Lisa opened her mouth. "I think you've got rather a lot to catch us up on, Isabel!"

And just like that, I was back in the circle.

Bonnie had said she would get out at the

beginning of the week, but though she'd been buzzing at the idea of freedom when I'd visited last Sunday, I hadn't given up on the idea that the doctors would back out of their decision. At the very least I had hoped they would delay her release by a few more weeks, just until things blew over and they could be sure the meds were working for her. Which was why, when my doorbell rang at lunchtime, I'd been taken aback to find her standing on my doorstep, suitcase in hand.

"Bonnie! What on earth are you doing here?" I spluttered, standing aside so she could slide past me.

She twisted her mouth, frowning. "Not quite the welcome I was hoping for. I thought you might come and pick me up."

"You've been discharged?"

"I told you I was going to be."

"I know you did, but I thought..."

"You hoped they'd change their mind. Sorry to disappoint."

"Oh, don't be like that." I glanced behind me as I shut the front door, relieved to see the reporters absent from their post. They hadn't given up hope of getting a statement from me yet, they'd been there an hour ago, but perhaps they'd gone for lunch. I was sure my stoic silence was boring and frustrating for them, waiting around in the cold all day only to be blanked when I passed them.

Bonnie walked into the living room and slumped down on the sofa, stretching out her limbs like a cat. "Where's Sophie?"

"At school. She'll be home in a few hours."

Bonnie nodded. "So what's new?"

"Nothing. Nothing's new." I eyed her suitcase, suspiciously. Bonnie didn't really have a place of her own, she'd hopped from one friend's sofa to the next over the years, but more often than not, when she got out of hospital she would hole up in my spare room. The idea of her being here while I was dealing with reporters, prank calls, stalkers – it just wasn't going to work. She needed peace. Calm. Not stress and cameras in her face. Telling her that she couldn't stay, without providing a decent reason was certain to set her off, but there was no other option. I would have to piss her off to get her to leave.

"What's that?" I asked, pointing to her case.

"My stuff. Obviously."

"I mean what's it doing here? You just assume you can move in without even asking. Don't you think that's a bit rude?"

"Um, no?" She sat up, glaring at me. "I was under the impression you wanted to help me. You're my sister, since when do I have to ask?"

"Since you pulled all that shit in front of my daughter last time. Coming in drunk and yelling at 4 a.m. bringing men back here, stealing my money. I can't have it, Bonnie, not with Sophie here. It's not fair."

"You know I only did that stuff because I was off my meds. I never meant to upset you, and I didn't bring men back here... Did I?"

In truth, it had only been once, and Sophie had been at school, but I wasn't going to concede that now. "Look Bon, I'm not blaming you. I know you only did it because you're ill."

"Were ill. Not anymore."

"Bonnie."

"Look at me, I'm better, I'm doing well. Why can't you see that?"

"I can, and I think you're doing amazingly. But you're always going to have it in you, Bon, it's there, it's a part of you."

"Don't you dare treat me like I'm some broken, defective piece of equipment, just waiting to implode. How do you expect me to move on with my life if you won't let me? If you keep focusing on what I did, who I was? Don't you get it, Issy? I'm ready to break out of that cycle. I'm not a fucking idiot, I know I can't just click my fingers, paste on a smile and be free of mental illness, but I *can* do this. I know I can. But you need to stop looking back and start supporting me in moving forward."

"I *do* support you. Of course I want you to be well. Look, why don't you go and ask Lucas if you can stay with him for a while, just while you get back on your feet. I've got a lot going on right now. Work stuff," I added hastily. "I just can't deal with any more responsibility at the moment."

"Oh, so you're going to pass me off to the brother-in-law then? I fucking knew you would do this eventually. Well, don't worry your busy little head about me!" she said, standing up and storming past me. She grabbed her case and spun to look at me. I could see anger in her eyes, but beneath that was hurt. "You're not the only one with an inheritance to burn. I'll rent a place of my own if it's going to be like that. I'll get out of your way, since I'm obviously a burden to you."

"Bonnie!"

"Fuck you, Issy."

She stormed out and I had to grip the door-frame to stop myself from following her. I was doing it for her, I had to remember that. Even if watching her go hurt my heart more than I could bear. I just hoped I hadn't pushed her too far already.

Chapter Fourteen

Being back in the office was both a relief and a nightmare. Bonnie hadn't called since we'd argued and Lucas had said she hadn't turned up at his. I hoped she was somewhere safe, that she wasn't so hurt by my rejection that she lost control again. If anything happened to her I knew I would never forgive myself.

"Isabel." I looked up from my computer to find Bill, my boss standing over me. "You okay?"

"Yes, fine Bill, fine."

"You sure?"

Bill was in his late fifties, and as bosses went, he was a good one. I liked that he mostly let me get on with my work without hovering over my shoulder, or tapping his watch if I came in a few minutes late, which admittedly was pretty rare. He could talk for hours about yachting, sailing around the Med and his plans for his retirement on his cushy Navy pension, but he wasn't the type for deep conversation. I could see from his stiff expression the effort it was costing him, checking up on me after *my little incident.*

"I'm fine, honestly Bill, being back here is just what I need. I want to be busy."

I saw the relief on his face as he realised I wasn't going to burst into tears, but then *that* would have shocked the whole office. I rarely got in a flap. I was sure they all expected me to sail through my recent stabbing incident without a single tear, or hair out of place. It was my own fault for painting myself as the ever calm, serene, capable caricature that I'd created, but I was grateful that people hadn't been too over the top with their sympathy, or made the assumption that I would need to talk about it. I didn't.

"Oh, that's good to hear," Bill smiled, his face relaxing. "Um, I've got Kelly out on a case, it's a nasty one and she might need to use you as a sounding board. It's only her third."

"What is it?"

Bill glanced at the sheet of paper in his hand, his smile fading. "Little boy, five years old. She's been round on a home visit and found him covered in cigarette burns and in a soiled nappy that hadn't been changed for a long time. Drenched in wee and poo, poor little chap. He's going to need skin grafts on his thighs and bottom."

"He's been removed?" I said, my gut twisting at the horror of it. That poor child. Those evil excuses for human beings who'd done this to him.

"Yes, taken to the children's hospital and he'll be placed in foster care immediately once he's been treated. Severe dehydration and malnutrition too by the sound of things," he tutted, shaking his head. "I'll have Kelly send over the paperwork for you to have a read. The father was arrested on the scene but they've yet to track down the mother. Not sure if she's even in the picture."

"Okay," I nodded, swallowing down my anger. I had to be professional now. Ensure I did everything in my power to support Kelly and make sure that this poor child never had to set foot in a room with his abusers again. "Thanks Bill, I'll get straight on it."

"Okay. And if you *do* need to chat, or feel like you need more time, just say. My door's always open," he said gruffly, his eyes trained on a spot on the wall. He was uncomfortable, but he was a good enough man not to let that stop him from making the offer.

"Thanks, Bill. I'll be okay. We've got children to help, I can't be worrying about myself."

He nodded and headed back to his office and I picked up the phone, dialling Kelly's mobile number.

I'd only just been on time to collect Sophie from school, I'd been so engrossed in the case. Horrible as it was, it was good to throw myself into someone else's problems again. Reading the paperwork and hearing about the details second hand wasn't the same though. I missed being there, right at the scene. Holding the child's hand, speaking the soothing words, letting them know they were safe now and seeing their expressions change as they realised I would help them. I had loved being a fairy god mother to them, being the one who got to save them. The face they would always remember.

As we pulled into the driveway, I was relieved to see no sign of the reporters. They hadn't returned since yesterday morning and I had a feeling they'd finally given up on trying to get a statement out of me.

"Those people aren't here, Mummy, the ones who want to take our picture."

"No, it doesn't look like it."

"Who are they? Why do they keep asking you things?"

I looked at her in the rear-view mirror, seeing the concern on her small face. "Just some very annoying photographers, baby. You don't have to worry about them."

"You don't like them."

"No," I sighed, putting on the handbrake and turning to face her. "But I find the best way to get rid of people like that is to ignore them."

"Like when Adam was pulling my hair in the playground?"

"Yes. Exactly like that. He wanted to get a reaction from you, didn't he? But you ignored him and he got bored and left you alone."

"Yes." Her voice was small. "But sometimes even if you're really quiet, some people still come and find you. Ignoring them only makes them more cross."

I looked into her wide brown eyes, knowing she still carried fuzzy memories of her old life. I held out my arms and she unbuckled her seatbelt, climbing into the front to sit on my lap, wrapping her arms around my neck. "Sometimes ignoring doesn't work, you're right. But it's always worth a try."

"But what do you do if they still won't leave you alone?"

"Fight back, I guess... show them they can't mess with you. And if you can't fight alone, accept help. Tell people what's happening."

"I'm glad you came to help me."

"Me too, sweetheart. You can always ask me to

help if you need it. Always."

"I know, Mummy. And I'll help you too."

"Thank you." I scooped her up, carrying her inside, her face snuggled into my neck as I breathed in the scent of her hair. "Go on up and get changed. I'll call you when dinner's ready."

She skipped upstairs and I went to get her bag from the car. She'd left the zip undone and half the contents were spilling out across the floor of the car. I scooped up her books and pencil case, shoving them back into the backpack and straightening up. As I turned, I was caught off-guard, a sharp slap ricocheting across my cheek. I stumbled back, hitting the car door, eyes wide as a short, obese and terrifyingly livid woman stepped closer, her face tilted up, her hazel eyes fixed on my own. I could see the spidery trail of bright red veins running beneath her eyes, across the sweating surface of her cheeks. Her thin lips were pulled into a tight snarl as she pointed a shaking finger at me. I had five inches on her, but her fury made me shrink back, and I knew instinctively who she was. They had the same square nose and dirty blonde hair. David's mother.

"You bitch," she growled, panting heavily. She slapped me again viciously, and my head was thrown to the side. "You killed my boy. My son!" I didn't know what to say. It was true. I'd killed her son, and if I were in her position I'd be just as furious. More even. "I don't know how you convinced them to let you go, but it's not right!" she shouted, specks of her saliva hitting my cheeks, making me recoil further into the cool metal of the car door. "You should rot in jail for what you did!"

"I didn't have a choice. It was self defence." I said, my voice strangely calm.

"Don't you dare! Do you think I don't know my own son? Know what he was capable of? He would never have done what you said he did! He used to pick up snails from the pavement and take them to the bushes so they wouldn't get stepped on. He carried the shopping in for me every week, because he didn't want me to hurt my back. He was a good boy – man. A really good man. And you took him from me!" She raised her hand to slap me again and I swung my arms in front of my face to protect myself. It didn't stop her though, she lurched forward, pummelling me with her fists, scratching and pinching the exposed skin on my forearms.

"Stop!" There was a blur of colour and the blows suddenly ceased, voices yelling shrilly. I looked up to see Bonnie separating us, her arms spread wide as she faced away from me, covering me with her body. "What the hell is this? What do you think you're doing?"

David's mum was bent over double, her hands on her knees as if she'd been the one getting the beating. She looked up at Bonnie and gasped. "You're kidding me? Twins? Oh that's fair, isn't it! You break my twins in two, take David from his brother, destroy our lives, but you've still got each other, haven't you? You've got your lovely big house, your perfect, happy lives. You don't know what it even means to lose something, you murderer!"

She couldn't have been more wrong, but there was no point in wasting my time trying to explain that to her. She wouldn't care anyway. But it seemed Bonnie had taken the comment to heart. I couldn't blame her. She stepped towards her, fearless and intimidating. Bonnie could be terrifying herself when she was pushed. "You are going to get off this driveway and go home, right now, or I'm going to call the police."

"I'm not the criminal here, your bloody sister is!"

Bonnie stared at her, not saying a word. Then she

pulled her phone from her pocket. "Last chance, old lady."

She glared back, then looked past her to me. "I hope he haunts you. I really do." She shoved her way past Bonnie and stormed out to the pavement. She got into a silver estate car with rusty hubcaps and a dent in the bonnet, not bothering to glance back as she revved the accelerator and sped off. Bonnie turned to face me.

I held up my hands. "I'm sorry, Bon, I really am. I didn't want you to find out like that. I can explain everything."

"I didn't find out like that." She took a step forward, frowning deeply. "Imagine my surprise when I was eating a bowl of mushroom soup, watching Loose Women and my own sister is the headlining topic. *Should we be allowed to kill intruders?* And a big bloody photograph of you. You're all over the TV, not to mention the internet!

Why didn't you tell me? Since when do we keep stuff like this from each other?"

I shook my head. "I'm sorry. I know, I just..." I put my head in my hands, breathing deeply. I needed to sit down. Before I fell down. "Can we go in. I need..."

Bonnie stepped forward, taking my arm and leading me to the door before I could even finish the sentence. She could read me better than anyone. "We'll go in and you can have a drink and calm down. But then you're going to tell me everything, okay?"

"Okay."

I didn't tell her everything. I couldn't. I told her just enough to keep her satisfied. David, the stabbing, the arrest, the reporters. Not the stalking though, nor the calls. Part of me wanted to get it all out in the open, but there was something stopping me. Fear that this wasn't necessarily connected. That it was more than just some pissed off relatives. I couldn't start dragging up the nightmares from our past.

"And you've kept all this to yourself?" she said, placing a hot cup of tea on the table in front of me and handing me a pack of frozen peas wrapped in a tea-towel. It made a change for her to be taking care of me, taking on the mother role that was usually mine. I wasn't sure I liked it.

"No, Lucas knows," I said, pressing the cool peas to my swollen cheek. "He's been really supportive. But you know what I'm like. I just want to move forward. Not focus on the past." She nodded, her lips pressed tightly together. "I was worried about you," I said softly, raising my eyes to meet hers. "When I didn't hear from you."

She shrugged. "I'm fine. I managed to rent a studio flat, just round the corner from here actually.

It's no good long term but it will do for now."

"I'm sorry I said you couldn't stay here, Bon."

"I just wish you'd told me why."

"I know. But you're doing okay?"

She smiled widely. "I am. I feel happy, you know? Like there's a world of possibility stretching out in front of me. I can't remember ever feeling like this. Wanting a real life for myself. Having dreams and hopes. It's a good feeling."

"It suits you," I grinned, standing up and glancing at the clock. "It's too late to cook. I'll order a takeaway. Why don't you go and say hello to your niece? If you're lucky, you might even get to see her doll do a wee."

"Just try and stop me," she laughed. She bounded out of the kitchen, light and free and happy and I smiled, hoping nothing would stop her from having the life she was dreaming of. She deserved it.

Chapter Fifteen

The doorbell rang for the second time in a row, accompanied by a hearty banging, and I rushed down the stairs, pulling the cord on my dressing gown, tying it tightly around my waist. The clock hadn't yet struck 7 a.m. and I wasn't expecting any deliveries. I had no idea who could be pounding on my door at this hour, but it couldn't be good.

Not that the ringing bell had woken me. I'd been lying in bed wide awake for hours, staring at the smooth plaster of the ceiling, unable to relax enough to drift off. I'd begun to have heart palpitations as soon as I lay down every night, my breath coming in short rapid bursts as my heart beat unevenly, choking me as it felt like it was jumping into my throat. It didn't make for a great atmosphere for sleeping. I fiddled with the lock, slid back the bolt and opened the door slowly.

"Morning," smiled Lucas. I took the ridged cup he was offering, smelling the delicious aroma of cappuccino.

"Hi," I managed. "Uh, do you know what time it is?"

He glanced at his watch. "Oh, were you sleeping?"

"No. Actually. But, it's early. What's going on?"

"Not a lot. I had to drop Oscar to the childminder's in the middle of the night because I was called in for an injured cat. Run over poor thing, but it died before I could save it." He said the words lightly, but I knew he'd be hurting over the loss of that animal for weeks.

"Oh, Lucas. I'm sorry."

He gave a shrug. "You'd think I'd be used to it by now, but I still find it hard."

"That's a good thing. It means you aren't jaded. You still care."

"I suppose so." He took a sip of his own coffee. "Anyway, there was a reason for me turning up at the crack of dawn. Other than to bring you coffee."

"Which is very welcome, by the way," I said, bringing the cup to my lips. He wrinkled his nose and I got the feeling he was about to deliver some bad news. "What?"

"On my way in last night I noticed something strange. I didn't have time to stop, and anyway, it was too late by then, but... well, come and see."

"See what?"

He held the door open, and I stepped outside, shivering in the chilly morning air. He pointed to my car and I saw instantly what he meant. I walked round it taking in the sight, feeling numb. The back tires had been slashed, and along the length of the driver's side, the word MURDERER had been scratched into the blue paintwork. "Oh."

"I know." He put an arm round my shoulder. "Look Is, don't you think it's time you called the police about all this? It's not on."

I shook my head. "I don't want them involved. There's no point, it will blow itself out."

"I'm not sure it will."

"They're just angry, that's all. I had David's mum here yesterday, shouting and screaming. They're just lost, grieving. It can't be easy for her."

"She came to your house?"

"Mmm. She needed to confront me, I suppose. Let all that pent up grief fly free."

"But they're taking it out on you, the victim."

"It will blow over. The garage I use around the corner will get this sorted. It will be like it never happened."

"But it *did* happen. Painting over the evidence is the worst thing you can do. You need to report this."

"I said no, Lucas. Just let me deal with this my way, alright?"

He took out his phone and snapped a picture of the car.

"Lucas!"

"I'm not going to do anything with it. This is just in case you change your mind. If things get worse."

"It won't get worse."

"I hope you're right."

I'd sent Lucas home to catch up on some sleep, then called the garage to come and pick up my car. I didn't think it was a good idea to try and drive it with the tires in such a state, and the thought of anyone spotting me in it was too humiliating to bear. The mechanic, a man who I'd used for every MOT and repair since I'd passed my driving test, had frowned silently as I'd shown him the state of the paintwork, my face flaming. Fortunately, he'd refrained from asking any awkward questions. He had promised to get it done before the end of the day if I paid extra, and I'd agreed without hesitation.

Once I was certain the recovery truck had gone and Sophie wouldn't see it, I walked her to school, feeling far less brave than I'd let on to Lucas. I didn't mind David's mum taking out her grief on me, it was understandable really. I could see her point of view. And now I'd seen the extent of her fury towards me, I was even more convinced that David's twin, Lee must be behind all the prank calls. Who else could it be? It made sense that they would blame me. It didn't matter to them what David had done, just that I had been the one to take his life. I just hoped they wouldn't try and cause a scene in front of Sophie. I didn't want her to be frightened. I couldn't be sure if she'd heard the confrontation on the driveway, but she'd been more subdued on the walk to school this morning and I knew I had to protect her from any more unpleasant scenes.

I actually felt relieved to have such a juvenile display of aggression directed towards me. It gave me cause to believe that all of the horrible things that had been happening lately were simply down to what had happened with David. Revenge, retaliation, whatever you wanted to call it. Nothing deeper or more sinister. My mind had been wandering to other explanations, but now I felt as though I knew what I was dealing with. And as I had said to Lucas, I was sure it would all blow over.

I rounded the corner into my road and crossed diagonally towards my house, wondering if I should go into the office late today. Maybe I should try and catch up on a few hours sleep first? I really did need it. Something caught my eye as I approached my driveway, pulling me from thoughts of my warm bed and feather pillows. On the garden wall were three long stemmed red roses, all laid out in a long line. Beautiful, perfect petals, picked right in bloom and left there for me to find.

I moved slowly towards them, staring at the smooth green stems, the sharp thorns jutting out from them. For a second, I couldn't move. Then, coming to my senses, I stepped closer, walking along the length of the wall, pushing each one over the edge into the abyss of shrubs and bushes in the muddy flowerbed. I turned away from the house, deciding not to go inside after all. I didn't need to sleep. I needed to work.

Chapter Sixteen

There was a glass of whisky on my bedside table and I didn't put it there. I stood frozen in the doorway to my bedroom, my mouth dry as I stared at the tumbler. I'd picked my car up from the garage at closing time last night, a sparkling new coat of paint and fresh tires erasing all evidence of the vandalism. I'd dropped Sophie to school first thing, and been halfway to the office before I'd realised that I had left the file I'd been working on at home, having taken it to bed with me the previous night. The case of the five year old little boy. If I had been getting any sleep, the reports coming in on this poor child would have been enough to give me nightmares.

I'd rushed home to pick it up and been halfway

out the bedroom when I'd seen the glass out of the corner of my eye. Now I wondered how I had ever missed it. The smell of the whisky filled my nostrils, bringing back memories I'd buried long ago. Memories of my childhood, my mother... and of events I wished I could scrub from my history. Someone had been here. In my house. My bedroom. The sheets on the bed were disturbed too, I realised as I looked closer. I felt sick. Violated.

With a sudden blaze of fury, I dropped the file on the carpet and rushed to the bed, determined to strip away the sheets, to boil them or burn them – I wasn't even sure. As I yanked a pillow from it's cotton case, the heavy silence in the house was broken by the unmistakable sound of smashing glass. I didn't think. I just reacted, running out of the room and down the stairs, adrenaline coursing through my entire body.

"Who's here!" I screamed. "Who's in my house?"

The front door remained closed and I sprinted past it, straight into the living room. The window was shattered, along with the glass coffee table. A brick lay among the debris, a note taped to its side. I didn't bother to read it. Instead, I ran for the door, grabbing the cricket bat I'd started keeping in the hall since David's death. Holding the bat in both hands I ran out of the house, my eyes darting left and right. A yell made me swing around on the spot and I was taken aback by the scene unfolding in front of me.

Lucas was grappling with another man as he tried to bring him down to the ground. The man was flailing wildly but there was no doubt that against Lucas, he was outmatched. With a grunt, Lucas swung him forward, pinning him face first against the pavement. He looked up at me, breathing heavily, his dark hair falling over his eyes. "I saw him throw a brick through your window... I was...

just... on my way to work."

I nodded wordlessly, walking towards them with slow, uncertain steps. Finally, I could end the mystery of who had been harassing me. Lucas kept his hands pinned on the man's shoulders as I squatted down, reaching forward and pulling the cap from his head. I sucked in a breath, shocked at being confronted with the spitting image of David so close up. It was like seeing a ghost. "Lee," I managed to choke out.

"Let me up!" he growled.

"So you can run?" Lucas sneered. "Not bloody likely."

I leaned back on my heels, using the bat to keep my balance. "You're the one who's been harassing me. Following me." He stayed silent, refusing to look at me. "Lee," I started, unsure of how to talk to a man who hated me so intensely. "I... I am sorry. I'm sorry you lost your brother. I can only imagine the pain you must be feeling right now."

Lee stopped avoiding my face, his eyes fixing me with a venomous stare. "Don't you dare talk to me about him. Don't you fucking dare. You're the reason he's dead."

I looked to Lucas who shook his head. "Go inside, Issy. Call the police."

"No. Not yet. Let me ask you something, Lee. Did David know everything about you? Every little secret?" He stared at me, his eyes blazing with hatred. I squeezed the rubber handle of the bat between my palms, digging my fingernails into it. "I bet you had secrets, even from him. And I know he had them from you, because you wouldn't be here otherwise. You wouldn't defend him so passionately if you knew... if you..." I shook my head, clearing my throat. "The bottom line is this. David threatened me, my child, our safety, and I had no choice but to do what I did. I'm a mother. I would do whatever it takes to protect my daughter. Can't you understand that, Lee? Do you have children?"

"A son."

"And what would you do if he was in danger?"

Lee stared at me and I didn't flinch away. I saw him mulling over my words, and then, the fight seemed to leave him in the blink of an eye. One moment he was like a captured animal, feral and vicious. The next he looked like a lost little boy. Lucas sensed the change in him and eased up slowly. He helped Lee to a sitting position and I saw that he was holding back tears. Then, just as if a switch had been flicked, he was suddenly sobbing, his chest heaving, all the hurt and anger he'd been carrying finally flowing freely as he gave into his grief. I felt Lucas's eyes on me, but I couldn't bring myself to look at him. I knew what he was thinking, the effort it must have taken him to stay with us. I knew he would be reminded of Roxy and the pain he'd lived through after she'd died.

"I just..." Lee sobbed, pressing the heels of his hands into his eyes, trying and failing to stem the tears. "I just needed a way to make sense of it. I needed someone to blame... someone to hate."

Lucas nodded. "Because focusing on that hate makes it easier to ignore the pain, doesn't it? But it has to stop now. You can't keep making Isabel suffer for this. She isn't to blame."

Lee glanced at me and I saw a flash of remorse. "I know." He swallowed back a sob. "I know you're right."

I reached out, touching his shoulder and he didn't flinch away from me. "I really am so sorry, Lee." He sniffed, wiping his nose on the sleeve of his jacket and I pulled a clean tissue from my pocket, offering it to him. He took it and I saw the acceptance as a positive sign. "We both need to leave this in the past and move on from what's happened. It's no good to keep living like this."

"I don't know how to move forward. How can I?"

Lucas cleared his throat before speaking, his deep voice cracking with emotion. "It's going to be hard, for a fucking long time. It will be one of the hardest things you'll ever do, so hard you won't believe you'll ever get through it. But you just keep putting one foot in front of the other. You keep living, and eventually you'll realise, it's not so painful anymore."

"How would you know?"

"I just do." He helped Lee to his feet and I wiped at my face, feeling hot tears dripping down my cheeks. It had been a long time since Lucas had spoken with such raw emotion about what he'd been through in losing Roxy.

Lee nodded, seeming to understand that the words carried weight, and the two of them shared an awkward handshake. He turned to me, not quite meeting my eyes. "I'm sorry. About the window. I'll pay to have it fixed."

"Thank you for the offer, but it's not necessary."

He dipped his head. "Okay. If you're sure. Bye then."

We watched as he walked away, shoulders slumped, hands buried in his pockets. He turned the corner, disappearing from our view and I let out a shuddering breath, leaning into Lucas as I swayed unsteadily. He took the bat from me and put his arm round my shoulder, kissing the top of my head briefly before leading me back to my house.

"It's over," Lucas said softly. "This whole mess. It's finished now. You can finally move on."

I nodded. "Thank you. For catching him. And for talking to him. The hardest part of all of this was not knowing who it was, writing to me, prank calling, following me. You know he broke in? He was in my room."

"Really?"

"Yes."

Lucas frowned. "We can still call the police. If you feel unsafe?"

"No. You saw him. He's not going to do anything, is he? He's just broken hearted."

"I think you're right. Grief does strange things to a person."

"Did you mean what you said? About it getting easier for you? Do you feel like you've moved on?"

He sighed. "She'll always be a part of me. I see her in Oscar, her mannerisms, her expressions. He lets me keep a little part of her. But yes, I've moved forward. I'm not lost to the grief anymore. I've accepted that she's never coming back and I'm not angry about it now. I've let Roxy go." He stopped at the front door, and I turned to face him. He was looking at me with his deep brown eyes and for the first time, I saw him not just as my brother-in-law, but as a man. A silence passed between us as our eyes met. He reached forward, brushing a curl from my forehead. "You'll be okay now."

"I will. I hope I will." His fingers lingered on the soft skin below my ear and I stepped back, breaking the contact between us. "I really should be going. I have to – "

"Me too." He dipped his head and turned away, striding up the driveway.

"Lucas," I called after him. He turned, smiling. "I really do mean it – thank you for stepping in."

"Anytime. You know that."

I watched him go. Then I went inside, closing the door but not bothering to bolt it. I swept up the broken glass, picking up the brick from the pile and glancing at the note attached to it. In red letters was the word "Murderer" scrawled across it. I threw it in the bin bag with the rest of the broken glass, called the local window fitter and then went to finish stripping the bed. Bundling the sheets under one arm, I carried them, along with the whisky glass downstairs feeling a lightness settle over me. I realised it was the first time I'd felt safe in my own home since the night of David's death.

Pouring the whisky down the sink, I breathed in, forcing myself to smell the tang of malt, refusing to be frightened by the memories it brought with it. I heard the post arrive and finished washing the glass before going to get it. My heart stopped as I saw it. A single red envelope, just like before. Only, this time, there was a name written across the front of it in wide black letters. *Belle.*

"No," I whispered, sinking to my knees, picking the envelope up with trembling fingers. "No!" I ripped open the envelope and opened the plain white card. A handwritten message was written on the inside.

Well done for dealing with the brother. Now it's just the two of us, darling Belle.

The card fell to the ground as I swallowed back bile. I had known. All this time, since that very first moment when I'd seen my face in the news, I'd known he would see it. And when he did, I knew he would come for me. I'd convinced myself I was wrong, pushed down the fear, told myself I was paranoid and for a moment, I'd even let myself believe it was all just Lee. A grieving brother taking his pain out on me for a little while. But now, there was no denying the truth. He was coming for me, and he would want to finish what he started.

Chapter Seventeen

1990

I padded into the kitchen, still dressed in my fluffy purple pyjamas, my feet bare on the cold, beige lino. It stuck to my feet with every step, and I wondered what it must be like to live with one of those mothers who actually cared about normal things like housework and cooking. I was always amazed when I slept over at friend's houses and saw how other families lived. Nothing like us.

I began to stretch my arms above my head, yawning widely, before stopping dead in my tracks. There was a man in the kitchen. He was pouring himself a coffee from the cafetière Auntie June had given mum for her birthday several years back. It had lived in the back of the cupboard collecting dust ever since then, and I realised that this stranger would have had to go searching to find it. The idea of him rifling through our cupboards made me feel uncomfortable. He had his back to me as he slowly eased down the plunger, and I wondered what he was doing here. He didn't look like the men mum usually brought back home with her.

The last had been an old guy in his fifties, with a handlebar moustache and a tattoo of a naked woman on his forearm. At first I thought he might be cool, but he'd quickly seen the complete lack of interest mum had in discipline or parenting in any form, and taken on the job for himself, deciding he needed to provide us with a "father figure." This had mainly involved him doling out punishments for any little crime he thought we'd committed, from "being rude" to asking too many questions. He'd hated to be questioned, and it hadn't taken me more than a few days to realise the reason was because he was entirely vacuous. There was nothing in his head but dust and archaic beliefs he didn't have the intelligence to challenge or change. He had grounded me, taken away my few meagre possessions and generally made life very uncomfortable. Mum, of course, had left him to it and never done a thing to stand up for me or my sisters. I'd been glad when he'd left. They always did in the end.

The man making coffee in my kitchen now though, was very different. For starters, he was only about twenty five, I guessed, though I wasn't great at figuring out how old people were once they got past about nineteen. He had dark, shining brown hair that looked freshly washed, a clean shaven, angular face and he was wearing a pressed pair of grey suit trousers, his white shirt open at the collar, revealing a smooth brown patch of skin. He lifted his head, noticing my presence, and broke into a warm smile, his dark eyes crinkling at the corners. He couldn't have been one of mum's flings. A man like him would never give her the time of day.

"Who are you?" I asked, folding my arms primly across my chest, very aware that the effect was somewhat ruined by the giant embroidered teddy emblazoned across my front.

"I'm Simon." He lifted the cafetière, nodding towards it. "Want some?"

"No, I'm only thirteen. I don't drink coffee."

"Your twin does."

"Bonnie?" I shrugged. "Bonnie does a lot of things I don't."

He raised an eyebrow, regarding me thoughtfully. "You sure I can't tempt you? It's a decent blend."

"No. Thank you. So, you're mum's new boyfriend or something then?"

He dipped his head, and it looked like he was hiding a smile. "It's early days. We're just dating at the moment."

"Oh. Okay." I was weighing up whether to tell him about mum's condition. I usually stayed well out of it, letting the men come to the conclusion for themselves. She wasn't good at hiding it. But she was going through a good patch at the moment, taking her meds, trying to make amends. I doubted Simon had any idea of the roller-coaster he would travel over the next few months if – no, *when* she stopped taking her pills, something she did on a regular basis without warning. I had a sudden urge to warn him, to give him the chance to get out now, but I decided against it. It wasn't worth my while to interfere, he could easily turn out to be just as bad as old handlebar moustache. I preferred to keep my distance with the men in mum's life. There was no point trying to be friendly, he'd be gone soon enough. I poured myself a bowl of cornflakes, sitting down at the table beneath the window to eat them in silence.

"Are you going to be here today?" Simon asked, his tone friendly.

"Yes. But don't worry, I won't be in the way. I have homework to do."

He came to sit down at the table, choosing the chair opposite me and I looked up in surprise. I'd expected him to go back upstairs to the bedroom. "Do you always spend your Saturday doing homework?"

I nodded. "I don't like to get behind."

"I was like that too. It feels good to get ahead of the schedule doesn't it? What do you have to do?"

"Uh, maths... and an essay for English."

"Which do you prefer?"

"English," I said without hesitation. "I love reading. I'm not quite as good at maths. But that's no excuse not to do well, is it? It just takes more work for me to get a decent grade."

He regarded me over his coffee cup. "It's unusual for a girl of your age to care so much about her studies. You've got a good work ethic, Isabel."

"How do you know my name?" I asked, a blush creeping up my cheeks at the compliment. I couldn't remember a time when anyone had paid attention to how hard I worked, or given me praise of any kind. It felt alien, and I wasn't altogether comfortable with it.

"Your mum told me. Anyway, as it happens, maths is something that comes easily to me. I'm a financial planner, so I'm pretty good with numbers. Very good actually. If you need any help, just come and find me, okay?"

"I... really?"

"Honestly. I don't mind." He sat back, sipping his coffee, relaxed, and I began to relax a little too. I watched him out of the corner of my eye as he scanned his newspaper. Maybe mum had finally found a nice one. It wasn't completely impossible.

Chapter Eighteen

Irritable didn't even begin to sum up how I was feeling. The office was lit up with florescent overhead lighting, trying to ward off the grey gloom filtering through the windows. Rain poured down in an unrelenting sheet, washing away the last few traces of the long summer. I shouldn't have felt sad. We'd been treated to far better weather than I could remember for years, it seemed ungrateful to complain now that it was over. But I couldn't help the feeling of darkness that seemed to have engulfed me.

After getting the card yesterday, I'd been desperate to get out of the house, escape to the safety and distraction of work. Only the window fitter had called to say he'd been held up, and I couldn't bear the thought of leaving the house wide open for anyone to creep inside. For *him* to. I knew he would see it as an invitation. He always did see invitations in perfectly innocent behaviours.

So I'd had no choice but to stay at home, worrying, pacing, checking behind doors and inside wardrobes. I'd put Sophie to bed early so she didn't pick up on the tension pouring from me, and then I'd spent most of the night alternating between patrolling the house, checking on locks and peering out of my bedroom window, dreading what I might see lurking in the darkness.

Arriving at the office had felt like a relief first thing this morning, but now the exhaustion, coupled with an overwhelming sense of fear was starting to get to me. I felt trapped. The paperwork blurred on the desk in front of me, names and dates muddling and merging. I'd never regretted taking the promotion when I'd adopted Sophie, it had felt right and the pace was far more suitable for the life of a parent. But now, I wished I could grab my coat and head out on a case. I needed to lose myself in someone else's problems so I didn't have to think about my own. I needed to fix something, be the kind of person who knew exactly what to do, how to protect others, the person I'd strived to be my whole adult life. But right now, I felt like the useless, frightened little girl I'd once been, the girl who could have done better, tried harder. And I fucking hated her.

I rubbed my eyes, then tutted, realising I'd smudged my mascara. Pulling a compact from my desk drawer, I wiped away the black smear and turned to Rebecca who occupied the desk opposite me. "I'm going to get another coffee. You want one?"

She wrinkled her nose, holding her mug in her hand, peering inside it. "Uh, I'm still drinking the last one you brought me. Is everything okay, honey?"

I nodded. "Yes, of course. I just had a bit of trouble sleeping last night. I'm feeling it today."

"I'm not surprised after all you've been through recently. I'd be wracked with nightmares in your shoes." I realised she was talking about David and nodded. "They aren't putting you through an investigation here are they? I was so worried they'd add to your troubles and suspend you or something."

"No. Bill said that since the case was closed and the police are satisfied, they won't need me to take a leave of absence."

"So you can get back to normal then. Not that it's something you'll forget. Some things just stick with you forever, don't they?"

"Yes. They do," I murmured. I plastered on what I hoped was a genuine looking smile and went out to the coffee machine before she could think of something else to add. She was right. There were some things you could never undo. Things you would pay for until the day you died. I knew that more than most.

The truth was, I knew how to keep a secret. I'd lived my whole life burdened by them. I knew how to keep those festering skeletons locked up, to push down that sick, nagging tension in my gut, and though they corroded me from the inside out I could never seem to let them free. Like the time I kept quiet when I knew my mother wasn't taking her pills. I kept that secret right up until the day she hung herself. Or back when Bonnie first started taking drugs and neglecting to come home. Lips sealed.

Some secrets can't be shut away forever, no matter how hard you try to bury them. They find a way out somehow, wreaking havoc, leaving devastation in their wake. But there are others that must never be shared. No matter how hard it may be, no matter how deeply they poison your mind, you can never tell a soul. I'd created a life to repent for my own secrets, to make up for all the wrongs I'd done. Somehow I'd made a life where I could almost believe I wasn't a monster. But now, since David, I couldn't seem to avoid those dark memories. I couldn't escape the person I had once been.

I lingered for as long as I could at the coffee machine, reluctant to go back to paperwork I knew I wouldn't complete, conversations I knew I'd dodge, yet I couldn't face going home either. Finally, knowing Rebecca would come looking for me if I took much longer, I sighed and headed back to my desk.

"There you are!" she grinned as I walked in. "This will cheer you up – look!" She pointed to my desk. There, right in the centre of the scratched wooden surface was an enormous bouquet of blood red roses. "Looks like it's not all bad, hey? So who are they from? I didn't know you were seeing anyone."

"I'm not." I gripped the coffee mug tightly between my palms, rooted to the spot. "They can't be for me," I said shakily, knowing even as I spoke the words that they were.

"The delivery man said your name. They're yours, Issy. You must have a secret admirer. Bloody wish he'd have a word with Kev, I can't remember the last time he bought me flowers." She leaned forward, her eyes sparkling in excitement. "Aren't you going to see if there's a note?"

"Oh... yes," I said, though I had no wish to touch the bouquet. Rebecca watched closely as I placed my coffee down on the desk and picked up the roses. They were heavy, two dozen at least. I turned the beautifully wrapped flowers in my hands, and there, tucked inside a burgundy satin ribbon was a small white card. I flipped it open. Just one word was printed inside, but it told me everything I needed to know.

Soon.

"What does it say?" Rebecca asked, leaning even further across her desk in an attempt to get a peek. I tucked it inside my pocket before she could read it.

"It says, *Would you like to go to dinner?* It's from one of the policemen I met when I was taken in. He was really kind to me," I lied.

"Ooh, lucky you, a man in uniform!"

I nodded, feeling sick to my stomach. "I... I need to go to the bathroom. Too much coffee."

"You're not kidding," she laughed. I dropped the roses on my desk, grabbed my bag and walked straight to the ladies room. I locked the door, fell to my knees and threw up a sea of black coffee until my throat was raw.

Chapter Nineteen

Going home wasn't an option. There was no way I could face another night like the last, the long, unsettling silences broken by unexplained creaks and noises. The waiting. I couldn't risk what might happen. Under any other circumstances, I would have gone straight to Bonnie, or asked her to come to me. Despite our occasional bickering, she was the one person I could trust to make everything better. We would talk and laugh and comfort one another until my worries buried themselves deep in the recesses of my mind once again. But I couldn't talk to her about this. And I knew, if I went to her now, she would see straight through me, she would know I was keeping something huge from her. She would push and push until it came out and then no amount of joking around and drinking wine would make things better. I couldn't do it.

Instead, I swung the car into my driveway, ran in and packed a bag for Sophie and I, and was back in the car in under two minutes. I drove to Sophie's school and found her playing tag in the hall as her after-school dance group came to an end.

"Hi, Mummy!" she squealed, running across the hall and wrapping her arms around my waist. I loved that she wasn't afraid to show affection towards me in front of her friends. The cool years were yet to arrive and she hadn't been shamed by her peers for not giving me the brush off.

"You ready, sweetie?"

"Yes, what's for tea?"

"I'm not sure." I took her by the hand, leading her out to the car park. I couldn't help looking around as we darted between parked cars, my vigilance making me look more than a little paranoid. I closed the car door behind Sophie and got in the driver's seat, clicking the central locking. Only then did I relax a little. Sophie chatted non-stop as I drove, and though I was usually full of questions about her day, I couldn't seem to make my voice work now. I felt drained and exhausted, the constant tension wearing me down and breaking my spirit. We drove past our house without slowing, though I couldn't help but stare, wondering if he was in there hiding somewhere, waiting for us to return. I couldn't shake the fear that he was lurking somewhere nearby. The thought made the hairs raise on my arms, a shudder passing through my body as I pushed down harder on the accelerator.

"Where are we going?" Sophie asked as we turned the corner away from our house. I didn't answer as I continued to concentrate on driving. A moment later I swung the car onto the kerb and unbuckled my seatbelt.

"Wait here, baby," I said, jumping out of the car and clicking the central locking behind me. I ran up the path and banged my fist on the door, feeling silly and shaky, but knowing I had no alternative. Heavy footsteps approached and then the front door swung open. Lucas stood there wrapped in a thick white towel from the waist down, his wet hair dripping down his temples, tiny droplets landing on his broad, bare chest.

"Oh," I said, feeling the sudden blush spread across my cheeks.

"Isabel? What's up?"

"I'm so sorry to just turn up without calling."

"Since when do you need to call?"

"I..." I kept my eyes trained on his face, refusing to let them drift down to the glistening expanse of bare skin below. I couldn't remember ever seeing Lucas shirtless before, not in all the years I'd known him, and the realisation that he was naked beneath the towel made me inexplicably nervous. I swallowed and took a breath, pushing aside my pride and embarrassment. "Can Sophie and I stay here tonight? I'm having a hard time feeling safe at mine," I admitted.

His eyes crinkled in concern. "Of course you can. Is she in the car?" I nodded. "Go and get her and come inside. I'll just chuck some clothes on and I'll be right down. Oscar's playing in the garden, he'll be pleased to see you both."

"You're sure?"

He frowned. "Am I sure that you and my niece are welcome here? Yes. Always." He reached forward, cupping my chin, lifting it gently. "It won't be this difficult forever, you know? Things will get easier again."

I swallowed thickly and gave a quick nod. He let go of me and went inside, leaving me on the doorstep. I wished I could tell him the truth. That nightmares never really went away for good. That they may lie dormant for months, years even, letting you fall into a false sense of security, they may blur and fade, but they could never truly be over. They were just in hibernation, and one day they would return, presenting you with choices you didn't want to have to make.

I knew it was only a matter of time before I was given an ultimatum, and I already knew that when the time came, I would make the right choice. I wouldn't cower and give in like I had when I was a child. I was different now. I was stronger. And when he came to finish what he'd started, he would get the shock of his life.

I closed the door to Oscar's room softly behind me as I tiptoed out to the dark hallway. Sophie and Oscar had been so excited to hear we were staying the night, they'd spent four solid hours jumping around like a pair of chimpanzees who'd been given e-numbers. Oscar had been chock full of bravado, telling us that he never went to sleep before 11 p.m. but his heavy eyelids told another story. I hadn't made it past two chapters of their bedtime story before I'd realised they were both snoring softly, Oscar in his white and blue cabin bed, Sophie curled up like a toddler in the single camp bed beside him. I was glad the change in her routine hadn't unsettled her.

My feet throbbed and as I reached the bottom of the stairs I thought about slipping off my heels as I might have done if I'd been home alone. I knew Lucas wouldn't mind. In fact he probably thought it strange that I never took them off. But I couldn't bring myself to do it. The heels were an integral part of the costume I wore, the front I presented to the world and removing them made me more vulnerable than I was willing to accept. I sighed, looking down at my swollen feet and pushed open the door to the living room.

"Hey," Lucas smiled. He was sitting at the far end of the sofa, a glass of red wine in one hand, a book in the other. He put the book down on the coffee table. "Did they go off okay?"

"Yes. Sound asleep already." I sank down on the opposite end of the sofa.

"Wine?"

"Yes please."

He poured a glass and handed it to me, our fingers brushing for just a fraction of a second. I glanced at his face, wondering if I was imagining this new tension between us. We'd sat together like this, drinking wine, chatting comfortably a thousand times before, but now something felt different. There was a charge in the air. I was noticing new things – the way his broad chest looked in his thin cream jumper. The smell of his aftershave. I wondered if I was simply grasping for distraction and finding it in familiar, safe places. It wasn't like me to swoon over a man. I had never been the type of woman to need a relationship, or even *want* one for that matter. The few boyfriends I'd had, had been packed off the moment they tried to turn our fling into something more serious. I didn't want a boyfriend. A partner. Husband even. I took a sip of wine, and leaned into the back of the sofa, hitching myself up so that my shins were on the cushion. If I wasn't going to go barefoot, the least I could do was take the weight off my feet.

"So how are you feeling?" Lucas asked, resting his arm on the back of the sofa and watching my face closely.

I shrugged. "Unsettled. I thought it would get easier after confronting Lee, but it's not that simple," I said. I wished I could unburden myself entirely to him. Tell him that David and his crazy family were the least of my worries right now, but I couldn't. Not without revealing secrets I'd sworn to keep hidden. I couldn't do that. I tried to listen as Lucas offered words of comfort, and then as he told me funny stories about his work. The life of a vet was never dull, but it was difficult to concentrate on what he was saying. His deep voice was soothing though, and I felt myself relax a little as his words washed over me. The moon was bright and high outside the window and the small, dimly lit room felt safe and cosy.

"I'm just going to get another bottle," he said, standing up.

"Did we drink it all already?"

He grinned mischievously. "Looks like it." He walked out of the room and I could hear him banging around. A few seconds later he was back, bearing a bottle of Merlot. "Voilà!" he said, dropping down beside me on the sofa. He was so much closer than before. His thigh pressed against mine as he uncorked the bottle and I knew I wasn't imagining the frisson between us. Lucas and I didn't sit like this. Not ever. We'd always kept a respectable distance between the two of us. Air kisses and brotherly hugs. He was my sister's husband for God's sake! *My dead sister.* I shook the thought away but it remained there, bright and obnoxious. Roxy was gone. Forever. And she had loved both of us without condition right up until the day she died. She would have wished us both happiness, wouldn't she?

Lucas handed me a full glass and I took a gulp, leaning back against the arm of the sofa to create some space between us. "Do you feel calmer now? Away from where it all happened?" he asked, twisting towards me.

"Away from home?" He nodded. "Yes, I feel safe. I always feel safe here."

"I hope so." He reached forward, his fingers brushing through my hair. I saw a change in his expression as he grew serious. He was so close now, his full lips inches from mine. I knew I had to make a choice. If we did this, it would change our relationship forever. We couldn't pretend we were nothing more than brother and sister-in-law after crossing that line.

"Lucas..." I whispered. "I'm not sure if..." I didn't know how to finish that sentence. *If it's a good idea... If we should do this... If I'll be able to stop once we start...*

"I know. But I've wanted to for so long." He took the wine glass from my rigid grasp, placing it beside his on the table, linking his fingers through mine. The warmth of his skin against mine was all I could focus on. "Haven't you too?" he asked softly.

I swallowed. "Yes," I admitted. My head was swimming. I'd had too much wine to rein in my self control, to force myself to say no, when everything inside me was screaming yes. His dark eyes were hooded with passion in a way I'd never seen them before as he leaned closer, his breath falling on my face. He held his position and I realised he was giving me the final say. An opportunity to turn away and laugh, pretend it was all a joke and change the subject. To go on as we always had. But I couldn't.

I closed my eyes, letting the smell of his skin wash over me and when I opened them, I tilted my head, bridging the gap between us. And then, we were kissing. His lips were hot and urgent against mine and all the reasons why we shouldn't do this seemed to melt away. For the first time in as long as I could remember, I felt like I could let a man penetrate the locked box that was my heart.

Chapter Twenty

1990

I felt like I was in some sort of American sitcom where the whole family comes together to sit round the table at dinner time. This never happened at our house. Never. I couldn't remember the last time dinner had been anything other than beans on toast eaten on the living room carpet, cheap plastic trays balancing on our laps as we watched TV. Mum didn't eat with us. In fact, these days she rarely ate at all, preferring to get her calories through a strict diet of whisky and coke.

But tonight, not only were we having a proper roast dinner – the kind my friends bragged about on a Monday morning at school after their domesticated mothers had made lunch for the whole family – but we were eating it at the table too. I would have complained at the change in routine, only I was more than happy to let go of our slobby eating habits and embrace this new phase, no matter how short-lived it might be.

Mum was letting Roxy spoon potatoes and chicken onto her plate, smiling graciously and looking like the ultimate Stepford wife, with a green dress buttoned up to her throat, her flaming red hair brushed and clipped back neatly for once. She sipped her wine slowly, not throwing it back in one gulp as she usually would, and I couldn't help but wonder if Simon was to thank for all of this. I'd been disappointed enough times to know better than to get my hopes up, but from where I sat, for the first time I could remember, it seemed like I belonged to a real, proper family. A mother and father smiling warmly, a real home-cooked meal and the happy chatter of my sisters. I let myself send out a wish that he would stay. That mum wouldn't scare him off. That we would finally have a dad in our lives to love and protect us. Simon saw me staring at him and grinned, passing me the jug of thick, glossy gravy. "Here you go, Belle. Dig in."

"Thanks."

"How was work today, love?" Mum said, sounding less and less like the woman I thought I knew.

"Really busy actually, Rosie."

"What do you do?" Roxy asked across the table, reaching for a second Yorkshire pud.

"I'm a financial planner."

"Oh."

"What's that?" Bonnie asked, barely stifling a yawn.

"Maths stuff. I enjoy it. In fact, Isabel here has asked me to help her with her homework for school."

"Oh, for Christ sake, Issy!" Bonnie exclaimed. "Don't tell me she made out she was struggling? Trust you to take advantage of the maths whiz!" she laughed through a mouthful of chicken.

I felt myself blush crimson, letting my hair fall over my burning face so they wouldn't see. Simon threw me an apologetic smile, realising his mistake. "It's really okay, I don't mind. And not everyone finds maths easy, it's nothing to be ashamed of."

"Did she tell you she's not good at it?" laughed Mum. "She's thirteen and she's taking her GCSE's with the year elevens!"

"Yeah," Bonnie smirked. "She's a fucking genius." Mum didn't even blink at the profanity. "She doesn't need a tutor. She needs to learn to relax."

"Is this true, Belle?"

That was the second time he'd called me that. I

couldn't remember anyone ever calling me it before, and I liked the way it sounded. "Well, I suppose I'm not awful at maths. I never said I was. But there are things I do have difficulty with."

"You're just pissed off that you're not the top of the class yet, even though they're three years older than you. Not to worry, give it a month and I'm sure you'll be there," Bonnie kicked me under the table playfully. "She got an A *minus* last week," Bonnie teased. "Oh, the horror!"

"Can you imagine the humiliation?" Roxy laughed joining in, though she gave my hand a squeeze to show she was only messing around. I was used to their teasing, it was all meant in jest, but with Simon listening in I felt embarrassed.

He was looking at me curiously. "You have high standards for yourself, Belle. That's nothing to be ashamed of. You're going to make something of yourself."

I blushed even harder, not used to getting praised for my achievements. "I'm not sure about that."

"Well I am. And I'm never wrong." He threw me a cheeky wink and I felt the tension melt away. I really hoped he would stay with us. He was exactly what this family needed.

Chapter Twenty-One

1990

I pushed my key into the front door as quietly as I could manage, desperate not to draw any attention to myself as I slipped inside, closing the door softly behind me. My chest was heaving painfully, the pressure of holding back the sobs that were trying to force their way out, making my breathing tight and shallow. I could feel a hot, sticky trail of blood dripping from my lower lip, and my right eye was already swelling massively. I squinted, wondering if that was normal. It wasn't as if I'd ever been in a fight at school before. I'd seen plenty. At the first shout of *Fight!* everyone would drop whatever they were doing, lunches left to go cold, football games abandoned as the whole of the school would swarm, forming a wide circle around the two contenders locked in battle.

Usually it was the boys, but I'd seen a few girl fights too. Either way, there was almost always one of the pair who I could see didn't want to be there. Would rather be anywhere else, but somehow had found themselves in the spotlight. More often than not, the adrenaline would kick in and hemmed in by the bloodthirsty onlookers, with the option of flight removed they would fight back. The teachers would stampede through the tightly packed ring, dragging the pair apart before any real damage was done, though I'd heard from Roxy's friend, Leah, that in her cousins school, one boy had been stabbed in the eye with a pen. But in our school it was mostly bravado. Still, the call of *Fight!* made the hairs raise on my arms, fear and excitement pouring through my veins as I joined the throng, unable to resist the spectacle.

Much as I liked to watch though, I'd have hated to be centre stage, fists waving as the crowd screamed on. Yet, it would have been preferable to what had happened to me today. I still couldn't get my head around it. I'd never done anything to draw attention to myself. I'd put my head down and got on with my work. I had a handful of people I could call acquaintances, mostly year elevens now that I'd been moved up to the top year, but there were a couple of girls I was still friendly with from year eight. Not really friends now, I didn't have time for that anymore, but people I had once been close enough with, to go to tea and sleepovers at their houses. Never mine, of course, not with the state of our domestic affairs. As time had passed and I'd put more effort into my homework than my friendships, they'd become not much more than acquaintances. People I knew just enough so that I could stand with them at break time and not feel too awkward. I'd never been bullied, people didn't seem to notice me enough for that.

Which was why, when a group of five year eight girls from my old Science and English class had surrounded me on my walk home from school, I hadn't even seen it coming. Hadn't been ready to fight, or run. At first I'd even thought they might have mistaken me for someone else. What possible reason could they have for being angry with me? But I didn't get a chance to voice any of it before they launched themselves at me. And this had been no show of bravado, they hadn't held back as they punched my face, pulled my hair out in clumps, and when I'd fallen to the ground, two had come forward, kicking me in the stomach, the ribs, stealing my breath from me. I'd curled tightly around myself, holding back the tears, shaking violently as they laughed. One of them had spat on my face, and I thought that might have been worse than the beating. It made me feel like dirt, like someone unworthy of kindness. It made me so angry I wanted to kill them. See how they liked it. Spit on their stupid faces. How dare they treat me like I didn't matter.

I'd waited until I was sure they'd gone, then dragged myself up, hobbling home as fast as I could. I didn't want anyone to see me like this. I couldn't bear the thought of having to explain what had happen, what they'd done. I was ashamed, humiliated and all I could think of was washing away the blood, hiding myself away so nobody would ever know. I stood with my back to the door, listening for sounds of movement in the house. Nothing. With any luck Bonnie and Roxy would still be out with their friends and Simon would be at work. It was just mum, somewhere. I wondered what she'd say if she saw me now. Suddenly, my embarrassment didn't seem to matter. I just needed to fall into her arms and be comforted. I needed her to tell me she would fix this. Go into the school and cause a scene. Stand up for me, like parents were supposed to do.

"Mum?" I called, hearing the waver in my voice.

"In here," she called back from the living room. I hesitated, the embarrassment building up again, but before I could change my mind, I lifted my chin and walked towards the living room. I pushed open the door and stepped into the room. Mum was flicking through a box of old photos, tossing them in piles on the carpet surrounding her. There were boxes upturned everywhere, and barely anywhere to stand. She didn't look up.

"Mum," I said softly, willing her to help me. She glanced up and her frantic sorting stalled.

"What have you been doing?" she shrieked.

"I – I was beaten up," I said, tears welling in my

eyes. It hurt to cry, the skin swollen and bruised.

"What for?" she asked, not moving from her spot on the floor.

"I don't know. I don't really know the girls. They were from school." A hollow feeling began to grow in the pit of my stomach. There was no flicker of emotion in her eyes, no concern or sympathy. Just cold hard blame. She was supposed to get up, put her arms around me, tell me I didn't deserve this, wasn't she?

"Well, you shouldn't be hanging around in those crowds. I'm always telling you not to mess around with those sort of girls." She wasn't. And I didn't. But I could see there was no point in arguing.

"Aren't you going to ask if I'm okay?"

"Oh for heavens sake, can't you see I'm in the middle of something important? Can't you see all this?" She gestured widely to the room, her eyes already leaving me, looking back to the box of photographs. I stood, silent, watching her as she began riffling through the contents once again, her hands moving fast as she muttered to herself. When after a minute she didn't look back up, I slipped quietly out of the room and walked upstairs. I went to the bathroom, leaving the door open and sat down on the side of the bath. I knew I needed to clean off the blood, put antiseptic on the cuts, but I felt too drained to even move. Instead I put my head in my hands and let myself sob. It wasn't fair. None of it.

"Belle?" came a soft voice from the doorway. "Oh my god, what happened to you?"

I looked up, shocked. "Oh, I didn't know you were here, sorry Simon," I said, my cheeks burning at the thought of him seeing me like this. I wiped at the tears, wincing. He stepped into the room, pushing the door closed behind him and crouching down in front of me.

"Sorry? Don't be silly, Belle, what happened? You're hurt."

I nodded. I tried to speak, but the words wouldn't come. I shook my head, a lump in my throat and then I was sobbing again. I tried to fight the tears but I couldn't seem to stop them. The sympathy in his eyes was overwhelming. Somebody cared. He brushed the blood crusted hair from my eyes, then lifted my hand, inspecting the cuts and bruises, a deep frown on his face. Then he leaned closer, wrapping his arms gently around me. "It's okay, sweetheart, it's going to be okay. Let it all out."

And I did. I sobbed into his shoulder, wrapping my arms tightly around his neck, breathing in the comforting smell of his aftershave. He was wearing a soft, cashmere jumper rather than his usual suit and shirt, and he had a fine layer of stubble over his chin that wasn't usually there. "Why aren't you at work?" I sniffed, pulling back after I'd cried myself out.

"I decided to work from home today. Your mum is, well, she's not her best."

I nodded, giving a short giggle. "I know. I saw."

He studied my face. "Tell me. What happened?"

So I did. I told him everything, even how I'd been spat on. I couldn't seem to let that part go. When I finished, he gave a grave nod. "You did nothing to deserve that, Belle. Nothing. Don't let it change you. I mean it. You're clever and beautiful and you're storming ahead of them, leaving them behind. And they know it. They're jealous."

"You really think that's why they did it?"

"I know it. And you don't need to be afraid, because this won't happen again. I'm going to make sure of that."

"You're going to go to the school?"

"I'm going to get it sorted. You know who these girls are? Their full names?"

"Yes, but – "

"I'll deal with it. I promise. But first, let's get you cleared up. You look like something out of a horror movie," he winked.

"Simon, you don't have to..."

"I know. But I want to. Someone has to take care of you. And your mother..." he gave a sigh.

"I can take care of myself," I said in a soft voice, blushing fiercely at his attentions.

"I know you can. But you don't have to while I'm here." He took a clean flannel and ran it under the tap until it was warm, then rang it out and brought it to my cheek. "I hope this doesn't sting too much."

It did, but I held my breath and let him wipe away the dirt and blood, biting my lip to stop myself from crying out. His eyes were soft as he wiped away the layers of dirt, his fingers moving my head gently to the left, and then the right. He rinsed the flannel again and took one of my hands, gently dabbing at the cut that ran along the back of it. I'd scraped it as they had dragged me along the pavement when I'd tried to scramble away. Tears came to my eyes at the memory of it and I shook them away. "So," I said, needing to talk to distract myself. "You said, *while you're here*. Does that mean you'll be leaving... one day?"

He stopped what he was doing, looking up at me, his expression serious. "Do you want me to stay?"

"I..." I shrugged.

He gave a smile, squeezing my hand in his. "I think you lot need a man around the house, someone to take care of you, don't you?"

"I always wanted a dad," I admitted.

He pursed his lips, appraising me, then gave a short nod. "I expect you've felt very alone. But you can rely on me. I'll take care of you, Belle. I'll stay, as long as you want me to."

"Do you mean it?"

"I promise." He pressed a kiss into my palm. "You need a bodyguard. I'm your man." He leaned across me, pushing the plug into the bath and turning on the taps. "I'm running you a hot bath. You need to take tonight off your coursework. Have a long soak and I'll make you some dinner in a little while. But right now, I'm going to go and deal with these girls. Will you be okay on your own?"

I nodded. "Yes, I think I will. I feel less panicky now."

"Good." He stood up and cupped my chin, tilting my face up towards his. "You're going to get through this, Belle. You mustn't let it harden you. Don't let them take away the sweet girl we all know. I'll fix this."

"Thank you," I said, believing him. Feeling for the first time in my life that I had someone who would go the extra mile for me. Stand up for me. He kissed me on the forehead, and guided me to my feet.

"I'll see you soon. Relax."

I nodded, and he slipped out of the bathroom, closing the door behind him. He was right. Those girls had done what they did because of them. Their issues, and maybe even their jealousy, not because of me. I couldn't have done anything to stop them. And I knew Simon wouldn't come back until he'd talked to their parents and made sure they wouldn't touch me again. I stepped into the hot bath, wincing as the water ran over my wounds, letting the water wash away the aches and pains.

Chapter Twenty-Two

1990

I sat on the edge of the double bed Bonnie and I shared, having dressed in my pyjamas after a long soak in the bath. It had helped a bit, but when Roxy had caught sight of me coming out of the bathroom, I'd felt the shame wash over me once again. I hadn't wanted to go over the whole story with her, it was too hard to force out the words, *I was beaten up, I don't know why.* Instead, I told her to go and ask Simon, and said I wanted to be alone. Now I could hear music playing downstairs, Madonna, so Bonnie must be home, but she hadn't come up. I felt tired, like I could crawl into a cave and stay there for six months. It was still hard to understand how anyone could be so angry at me to want to hurt me so badly. I couldn't remember the last time I'd even spoken to those girls. I stared at the carpet, my ribs hurting with every breath. By the intensity of the pain, I was pretty sure they were broken.

A quiet knock sounded at the door and I was about to shout for whoever it was to go away, when Simon pushed it open, stepping inside.

"Hey you," he said. "How are you feeling?"

"Not good," I answered, not meeting his eyes.

"You not coming downstairs for dinner? I bought Chinese, your favourite."

"I'm not hungry."

"I'm not sure that's true." He sat down beside me on the mattress, his leg pressed against mine as he took my hand, holding it gently between both of his. "You have nothing to be embarrassed about, Belle. This wasn't your fault."

"Did you speak to their parents?" I asked,

looking up at him.

"No, Belle. I didn't speak to their parents."

"Oh." The disappointment was like swallowing a rock, sitting cold and unmoving in the pit of my belly. I'd really thought he would help me. I'd trusted him.

"Hey. Don't look so sad. In my experience, going to the parents is about as useful as going to talk to the school. Everyone gets in a big flap, talks a lot about how they're going to fix the situation, how it's totally unacceptable, but nothing actually gets done. Meanwhile, the bullies are pissed off that you've grassed on them and take their anger out on you. It's a waste of time and it won't help. It only makes things so much worse."

"You mean we do nothing," I said flatly.

"Nope. I mean we cut out the middle man. Go right to the source and cut it off there."

"So... you went to see the girls themselves?"

He nodded. "Exactly."

"I'm not sure that was a good idea. You could get in a lot of trouble."

"I said I'd stand up for you, protect you, didn't I?"

"Yeah."

"Well, that's what I've done. I found the girl who spat on you first, since it sounded like she was the ringleader. She won't be bothering you again. You can be sure of that."

"Really? How do you – "

"Then, I found three of the other girls at the park round the corner and dealt with them. The last one, the one you said kicked you when you were on the ground, she was at home but her parents weren't back yet."

"You just spoke to them?"

"Mostly. I had to act tough, you know, scare them off properly," he grinned. "We don't want them thinking they can mess with my girl again."

I blushed, smiling. It felt unbelievably nice to know he was on my side. "Thanks, Simon. Nobody has ever gone out of their way for me like that before. Did you find out why they did it? Why they hate me so much?" I was embarrassed to ask but I needed to know, to try and make some sense of it all.

"Jealousy. As I suspected. The kicker, Sara, is in trouble at home for not doing her schoolwork. Apparently her mum keeps asking her why she can't be more like you. She's impressed that you were moved up early and Sara said if you weren't such a show off, her mum wouldn't be so tough on her. The girl who spat at you told me that there's a boy she likes in your maths class but he's only interested in you. She thinks you've got an unfair advantage being in with the older kids."

"What? I don't think so!"

"You haven't been talking to any boys? Had them flirting with you?"

"I doubt I would notice if they were. I don't even know who she means."

"Good. Of course, I'm not surprised. You're a thousand times prettier than phlegm girl is, but still, I don't want those year eleven boys thinking they can take advantage of you."

"They don't." I sighed, relieved that he'd gone out and found them. Who knew what they would have done next if it wasn't for him.

"The other three were just along for the ride," Simon added. "They didn't have their own grudges, just got dragged along by Sara and Phlegm."

"Louise. Her name's Louise," I said, giggling. "Do you really think they'll leave me alone now?"

"They won't even look at you. I promise. I may have come down a bit hard on them, but I didn't want to take any chances."

"You... you didn't hurt them?"

"Nothing they won't survive," he grinned. I couldn't decide if he was joking or not. There was a strange glint in his eye, but I realised I didn't care. After all, that's what dads did, wasn't it? Protected their daughters, went a bit over the top to keep them safe. And he had done it for me. And if he'd scared those girls, *good*. I was grateful for it.

"Belle," he said, squeezing my hand. "You are so sweet and pure, so much better than they'll ever be. Don't let what they did destroy who you are."

"I won't."

"Will you come down for some dinner?"

"Do I have to?"

"No. Not if you aren't ready. Why don't you get in bed and I'll bring you up a plate?"

"That would be good." I turned to get under the covers and let out a moan.

"What is it?" he said, his face a picture of

concern. I liked it.

"Just my ribs. They hurt. A lot, actually."

"Oh, Belle." He wrapped his arm around me, letting me lean on his shoulder. After a moment, he spoke. "Let me help you." With a swift, smooth movement he stood, lifting me up with one arm, pulling back the quilt and laying me down carefully on the pillows. "There," he said softly. "Paracetamol and Chinese food coming up." He kissed me on the forehead and headed for the door. I watched him leave the room and knew that everything would be alright, as long as he was with our family. Simon would take care of us.

Bonnie and Roxy had been subdued over breakfast in the morning. It was clear that Simon had filled them in on the details and obviously told them to keep their comments to themselves, but they'd been fussing around me like mother hens, bringing me tea and toast, asking if I wouldn't prefer to take a few days off. Roxy had told me off for putting my studies before my health, but I didn't want to sit around wallowing. I needed to keep my mind focused on other things, not keep replaying the events of last night.

Mum, of course, had been nowhere to be seen. Simon said she'd gone out late last night and hadn't got home until past dawn. None of us said anything, but we all knew what it meant. What was coming next. It was selfish, but I wished she'd wait. Just until the exams were over. I had enough to deal with without her giving me more to worry about. I shook my head, as if I could dispel the thought, disappointed in myself for even thinking such a thing.

Walking through the school gates, my long hair parted at the side, sweeping over my swollen eye in an attempt to hide it, I glanced towards the main hall. Outside the door stood three of the girls from last night. Josie, Louise and Amy. Sara and Leanne were missing.

My stomach dropped, my hands already starting to shake as the image of them surrounding me flashed through my mind. I couldn't stop remembering the sickening sound of bone on bone as their fists collided with my face and body. This was a bad idea. I wasn't ready to see them. What if Simon was wrong? What if they came at me again? Was I about to be in one of those public, humiliating school-yard fights, everyone screaming as they bore down on us, watching as they kicked me to the ground? I couldn't bear it.

I froze in the gate, one foot on school ground, the other ready to run, remaining on the pavement behind me. They had seen me, I could tell. But there was no anger on their faces. No knowing smiles. They were looking down at the ground, eyes studiously trained on their shoes. Maybe Simon had been right after all. Louise, the one who'd spat at me, broke away from the group and I stood like a deer in headlights, my fists clenching instinctively at my sides as she slowly walked towards me. One of the others called after her but she ignored them. She came to a stop in front of me and I gasped, unable to tear my eyes from her face. There was a huge purple bruise blooming across her cheekbone and her lip was split right through the middle. She looked just as bad as me, if not worse.

"What happened to you?" I asked, the words falling from my mouth before I could rein them in.

She raised an eyebrow and winced. "I – I just wanted to come over and say sorry. I shouldn't have done what I did. Especially the spitting. I won't come near you again, none of us will, okay? Tell your dad I said that, okay? Tell him I apologised."

"My dad?"

"Yeah, promise me you'll tell him? We'll leave you alone from now on, just don't let him come and find us again. You'll do that, won't you, Issy?"

I nodded silently and she turned, walking towards the others. They linked arms and hurried off, casting worried glances over their shoulders.

I realised I was blocking the gate and stepped inside, bewildered. Had Simon done that to her face? He'd said he had to act the tough guy, but I didn't think he actually meant he'd hurt them. He must have scared the life out of them, maybe threatened to come back, or else they'd have gone right to their parents and the police would have turned up at our front door. There was no way he could have gone half measures, they'd have to really believe he would come back for them, or they would tell everyone. Had he really gone so far? The idea of Simon acting tough was almost laughable to me. I couldn't imagine ever being scared of him. He was sweet and kind and caring. He would have really had to put on a show for them to believe he was a threat. But, he *had* been livid. Scared for me and worried they'd do it again. Was it any wonder he had been a bit extreme in his reactions?

I realised Louise had called him my dad. And I hadn't corrected her. It had felt good. Made me feel proud to have them think that he would always be there to stand up for me. As I headed for assembly, I smiled. So what if she was a bit hurt. So what if he'd scared them. They deserved it.

Chapter Twenty-Three

I was grateful for the incessant noise and chatter between Sophie and Oscar when morning arrived. It helped to mask the uncomfortable tension and atmosphere of guilt between Lucas and I. We'd kissed. I was still struggling to believe it. Not just a quick peck, but a full twenty minutes of making out on the sofa like lovesick teenagers. His hands had been all over me, his body pressing hard against mine and I had known how easy it would be to just let him take me to bed.

Instead, I'd somehow managed to get a grip on myself. I'd pulled away, leaving him staring after me as I made some stupid excuse about it being late and rushing off to the guest room. Fucking coward. I felt sick with embarrassment and shame over what we'd done, unable to stop picturing him and my sister, their beaming faces as they'd cut the cake on their wedding day. I was a horrible person.

I grabbed the children's backpacks and bundled their coats over my arm. "Sophie, Oscar, are you ready?" I called up the stairs. "It's time to go."

"They're brushing their teeth," Lucas said, appearing at the top of the stairs looking rumpled and tired. He was still wearing his pj bottoms and once again he was bare chested. I couldn't cope with this.

"Oh... okay. I thought I could drop them off at school on my way into the office. Give you chance to have breakfast in peace?"

"You don't want to walk them there together?"

"I don't have time. I've got loads to get sorted today," I said, making a show of rifling through Sophie's bag so that I didn't have to look at him.

He shrugged. "Okay. We'll catch up later, shall

we?" Oscar and Sophie appeared beside him, charging down the stairs.

"Sophie, come here, you've got toothpaste all over your mouth!" I said, shriller than I'd intended. I held her chin still as I wiped away the sticky mess with a clean tissue, Lucas's question hanging unanswered in the air. "Got your book-bag, Oscar?" He held it up in response. "Right, say goodbye to your daddy, we're going in my car today."

"Yay!" they shouted in unison, executing a messy high-five that barely made contact. "Bye, Dad!" Oscar yelled, pulling the door open and running outside. Sophie followed after him, leaving me no time to hang around. "I'd better..." I pointed after them, my words trailing off.

"Yes. I'll see you later then."

"Uh hu." I rushed outside after the children, not looking back to see if Lucas was still watching me.

The sun was low in the sky as we clambered out of the car. The long, light evenings were over and the blanket of darkness came earlier and earlier every day. It was a relief to finally be out of the office, the day had been long and painful once again. And though I hadn't thought it possible, it had managed to prove even worse than yesterday, because now I had nowhere to escape to. I couldn't go back to Lucas's house – I couldn't trust myself with him, and giving into that pull, allowing him into my heart wasn't fair right now. I came with way too much baggage. I couldn't hide behind him like some lost little girl. I had to face my problems head on. I knew exactly what I had to do. I had to go home.

I looked up at the house, my stomach churning, my bravado fading as I looked to the dark windows. I could still change my mind. Drive to Lucas's house, eat dinner and sleep over and let fate and feeling take over and decide my path. But I wouldn't do that. Sophie skipped up the driveway, a bunch of buttercups squashed into her sweaty palm, a gift from a new friend at school, and with a steadying breath, I followed after her.

I unlocked the front door, relieved to see it appeared untampered with, and pushed it open. The weight of the brand new bush-craft knife in the pocket of my black slacks pressed reassuringly against my thigh. Sophie darted in ahead of me and gave a squeal. "Ooohhh, look Mummy! A Valentines card for my baby." She picked up the bright red envelope from the mat, showing it to me. "Look! It says Belle."

I froze, my hands growing clammy, my heart pounding hard against my chest. "Give it to me," I said quietly. She handed it to me without a word. I stared at the neat, blocky writing, holding back tears.

"Will you read it to me, Mummy?"

"Not yet. It's a bit early for Valentines day, my darling. We've got Christmas to do first and that's not for ages. Someone must have been a bit keen. I'll put it away safely and we'll get it back out on the proper day." Sophie opened her mouth as if to argue, but then clamped it tightly shut, her eyes trained on her feet, disappointment written all over her pale little face. I hated that I'd lied to her, that she felt this way because of me. I wanted to scoop her up, open the card and make up some words to match her excitement, but I couldn't do that. She would want to see it, and though her reading had a long way to go, she could recognise plenty of words. Enough for me to know I couldn't risk it. I had no idea what I would find inside the thin red envelope.

I waited until she was safely out of sight, upstairs in her bedroom, then went into the kitchen, closing the door behind me. I ripped open the envelope, pulling out another plain white card, just like the previous ones. My hands were shaking as I opened it scanning the words, my face flushing.

I saw you. The whole show. You knew I was watching, didn't you? Are you trying to make me jealous?

It's working.

My turn next.

I felt numb. He'd been there. Lurking outside, watching me when I was at my most vulnerable. *This* was why I could never let go. Why I had to shut myself off from any emotion or desire. Why I had to stay vigilant. I'd been too slack lately. I'd let myself do stupid things.

Card in hand, I turned to the hob, pressing the button until the gas ignited, the bright orange flame flickering, ready. I held the card into the centre of the ring, ignoring the pain of the heat licking against my wrist as I watched his words disintegrate into nothing but ashes.

Turning off the flame, I pulled the small knife from my pocket, opening it, seeing the glint of the razor sharp blade. I'd paid cash. The bearded, dreadlocked man in the shop had told me it was the best you could get for bush-craft. The only one he ever used when he wanted to fillet a rabbit. He'd remarked on my outfit. Smart black slacks, red silk shirt and my trademark stilettos in matching red. Told me I might not get far like that. I'd forced a laugh and said that he wouldn't recognise me on the weekends – that this was all for work.

I wouldn't use it. Of course not. Not again. But it made me feel safe to carry it with me. To know that

I could defend myself and my daughter. We weren't going to be victims. The doorbell rang, and I braced myself, slipping the weapon back into my pocket and taking a breath. I walked slowly down the hall, standing on my tiptoes to look through the little window on the door, and breathed a sigh of relief. "Bonnie!" I exclaimed opening the door, letting her inside.

"You seem surprised."

"No, just pleased to see you is all." I wrapped her in a tight hug. "Are you okay?"

"Yes. Are *you*?" she pursed her lips, frowning.

"Uh hu, come on, I'll put the kettle on and you can tell me about life as a free woman."

"Very funny. I wasn't in bloody prison you know."

"I know, sorry. I don't know why I said that." She frowned again and followed me into the kitchen, pulling herself up on a barstool at the breakfast bar. "So," I said, before she could ask me anything. "How are you?" She looked well. There was a freshness to her face that was new, a sparkle behind her eyes that looked natural. Healthy rather than manic.

She grinned widely and I was taken aback. It had been a long time since I'd seen her like this. "Really good," she answered. "I've got myself a job."

"Already? You sure that's a good idea?"

"It feels like the right thing to do. I want to be busy. Productive. I don't want a load of empty time to fill, you know?"

"Yes. I know. So what's the job?"

"Don't laugh."

"Bonnie, as if I would. Go on, tell me."

"Okay. Well it's nothing special. It's a receptionist job at a tattoo studio. The one I go to to get mine done, actually. I was in there last week getting this," she said holding up her hand for me to see. I took her hand, looking at the design on the back of it. It was a wide, turquoise butterfly, deep blue shading blending out towards the edges of it's beautiful wings. I stared at it, trying to find the hidden details. Bonnie always hid her darkness wrapped up in the distracting layers of beauty. There was always another, more disturbing side if you looked closer. But this time, hard as I looked, I couldn't find it. She held her silence as finally I raised my eyes to her face.

"What does it mean?" I asked softly.

"Transformation. Freedom. Saying goodbye to the person I was and embracing the next stage. I know the butterfly is a little cliché. Overused. But it's perfect for me right now."

"Bonnie... I love it." I said. I held back all the other thoughts that came to mind. I wanted to tell her that although I loved her determination, getting better was not necessarily going to be a straight path. She would fall and struggle and go back and forth and zig-zag her way to mental health. But I didn't want to rock the boat. She was trying and that was better than she'd done for years. I would keep my silence and be there for her when she stumbled.

"So," I said, letting go of her hand and dropping teabags into thick ceramic mugs. "A receptionist at one of your favourite places. Why would I laugh at that? It sounds perfect."

"Well, because Shane, the guy who runs the place, said that if I'm interested he'll train me up to do the tattoos. He's seen some of my drawings and thinks I've got what it takes."

"Seriously? That's fantastic! You have such an eye for art. And a creative job is just what you need. You loved the band before, didn't you?"

"I did. I miss it, but I can't go back to that now. I let them down too many times."

"You know they understood why."

"Maybe. But it doesn't make it okay. I didn't expect them to wait around for me forever – they've got a new singer now. I hear they're doing pretty well." I took her hand again and she shook her head. "I'm okay about it. Really. And if anything, it's taught me a lesson. I'm not going to throw away this opportunity now."

"You sound like you really want this."

"I do. I can't keep living in limbo forever. It's time I made something of myself." She grinned suddenly, her whole face lighting up. "Bonnie Cormack, tattooist to the rich and famous. Sound good?"

"It bloody does. I'm proud of you Bonbon."

"Ah, shut up, you'll make me blush."

"I doubt you know how!" I laughed. She'd never been the type to care what anyone thought of her, blushing was not in her nature.

"So, tell me what's new with you?" she smiled,

taking the tea I passed her and turning the tables on me. "I popped by last night and you weren't here."

"Did you?"

"Mmm. So?"

"Oh, I was just at Lucas's house picking up Soph. We went round for tea so the kids could play."

"Ah, rubbish. I hoped you might have a secret boyfriend we could gossip over. I've been single so long I've forgotten what romance is."

"So you wanted to live vicariously through me?"

"Something like that," she winked.

I turned my back on her, so she wouldn't see the truth in my expression, pulling a jar of rice from the larder. "You staying for dinner? I'm just doing a vegetable curry."

"Of course. So no boyfriend then?"

"Nope."

"And no secrets?"

Her voice was light but I knew she was probing

for more. Did she know something, or just sense it? I couldn't tell. I kept my back to her as I measured out the rice into the pan. I hated to lie to her. I would have loved to be able to tell her. To ask her what to do.

"Nope," I said. "Although I did spend three hundred pounds on a new coat. I suppose that should remain a secret."

"Can I borrow it?"

"Absolutely not."

It was getting late as Bonnie said her goodbyes. She'd read Sophie's bedtime story, and I'd joined them, sitting on the end of her single-bed, revelling in the sight of the two people I loved more than anything giggling together like they didn't have a care in the world. They had both been through so much, had so much thrown at them but to look at them now, you would never guess. They looked happy. Free. Bonnie and I had chatted long after Sophie had fallen asleep, and the more we talked, the more confident I felt that this time was different. She *wanted* to be better. That had to make a difference, to give her a better chance of fighting against her demons.

I'd drawn the curtains, conscious that I didn't want anyone watching us together, lurking outside in the darkness, but even through the thick velvet I could feel eyes on me. Several times I came so close to telling her everything. Stopping the conversation to beg for help. But I wouldn't be the one to steal this new found happiness from her. So I kept my mouth shut, occasionally running my fingers nervously over the little knife concealed in my pocket.

Eventually, she'd clambered to her feet and said she needed to go home. She was supposed to take some drawings into the tattoo studio in the morning and she wanted to finish the last one she'd been working on. I was sad to see her go, it had felt so good having her close. It always felt like together, we could tackle anything. It was stupid really since we'd failed at that so many times before. But she knew me better than anyone, and I her. Apart from the heavy secret weighing down on me, I could pretend for a little while that it was all going to be okay.

I watched her get in her car and waved goodbye, closing the door as she drove away. I went back to the kitchen and saw her purse laying on the table. Grabbing it I ran back to the door, flinging it open, hoping to catch her, but it was too late. The road was deserted. I sighed.

I was just pulling the door closed when I saw it. A wrapped box, long and thin, laying on the ground in the centre of the porch. It hadn't been there when Bonnie had left moments before. I knew it hadn't.

She would have tripped over it. We would have seen it. My blood ran cold as I realised that whoever had placed it there was still nearby. Watching me. I grabbed it, and ran inside, slamming the door hard and locking it, sliding the bolt across. I didn't pause as I ran to the back of the house, checking the back door lock. I dropped the box on the breakfast bar and raced up the stairs to Sophie's room. The soft glow of her night-light illuminated her face, peaceful in sleep, her body curled round her baby Belle. She was safe. It was okay.

With a feeling of walking to my own execution, I went slowly down the stairs, back to the kitchen. The box was light, and beautifully wrapped. Peeling back the paper, I saw it was from a jeweller in town, a one off place that I loved for it's unique pieces. Trust *him* to ruin that for me. I'd never be able to set foot in the place again without thinking of him standing in the spot where I stood, running his hands over the polished wooden display cabinets. I flipped back the lid of the box. Inside was a golden, heart shaped locket set on a delicate chain. I opened it cautiously, not wanting to see if there was a picture inside, yet unable to stop myself. As I eased it open though, I discovered no picture. Instead, nestled inside it was a tiny, folded note. With a sinking feeling I unfolded it, laying it flat to read the words.

Belle. I'm a forgiving man. You know that more than most. And you know how patient I can be. That's why I never gave up. You've not made it easy. I can't believe you changed your last name! You always did like to play games, didn't you? You liked to tease. But now I've found you, I'm growing tired of the chase. I've waited too long.

I know you're already regretting that kiss. I know you don't want him. You want me.

Sam Vickery

I'll come for you soon.
And we can finally be together.

Chapter Twenty-Four

1990

"Bonnie, I am not going to wear this!" I squealed, looking myself up and down in the full length mirror in our bedroom. Almost a month had passed since I'd been attacked by those girls and my bruises had finally all gone. True to their word, they hadn't bothered me again.

"You bloody are. You look gorgeous."

"I feel ridiculous." I twirled a half circle so I could see the low back of the dark green mini-dress Bonnie had got for me. I knew she had no money, so it was pretty much a given that it was shoplifted. The dress was clingy, a sheer Lycra material that moulded to my new curves. Bonnie had got breasts first, of course, but I'd been grateful it had been her rather than me. I wasn't ready for my body to change. I didn't want to leave my childhood behind me.

Bonnie didn't seem to mourn the loss of *her* childhood, but then why would she? She'd always been five steps ahead of me when it came to everything, bar school. She'd been desperate for her body to match her mind, to flaunt her new grown up curves to everyone who cared to look. But though my breasts had taken six months longer to arrive, when they'd come, they were actually bigger than hers. Not huge like some of the girls in our class, who I couldn't help but stare at when we got changed for PE, but still, they were full, round B cups and against my narrow waist they were hard to miss – especially in this dress.

"I look like I'm twenty. Are you sure everyone else won't be wearing jeans?"

"Who cares if they are? We want to stand out, don't we?"

"No."

"Oh, don't be such a spoil-sport, Issy. For once, can't we just do things my way? You're too uptight babe, it's time you found your wild side." She opened her bedside cabinet and pulled out a bottle of Jack Daniels. "Here. Have some."

"That's mum's!"

"I think you'll find she has more than enough to keep her going. Go on. Have some."

I took a tiny sip as Bonnie watched me. I knew she'd been drunk before. Plenty of times actually. But while she'd been sneaking into house parties for the past year and a half since we were eleven, I'd always opted to stay home and work on my coursework. I wasn't going to pass my GCSE's and get into college early by acting like a reckless child.

"More," Bonnie pushed. "Take a big gulp. You

need all the help you can get to loosen you up."

I frowned at her. "You know, I *can* change my mind. They won't let you in without me." The party was being held by one of the year elevens. I was sure she'd only invited me out of pity since she was inviting the whole class. I doubted she'd ever expect serious little Issy to actually come. But of course, when Bonnie had heard about it, there had never been any question of us not going.

She screwed up her face. "One," she said, holding up her index finger, glitter sparkling at the tip of her nail. "I don't know if you're aware of this, but we share the same face. I doubt you've talked to them enough for them to tell the difference between us. And two, *you* need to learn to relax. Play sometimes. It's *one* night, Issy. One party. You can go back to your boring coursework tomorrow, but tonight, just let go and enjoy yourself for once, okay?" She smoothed down her dress, a similar style to mine, except hers was bright red and cut more daringly between her pert little breasts. I could see that she wasn't even wearing a bra, her small nipples pushing against the fabric. She tilted her head to the side, waiting.

"Oh fine!" I exclaimed, knowing she would go on relentlessly until she wore me down anyway. I threw back my head and took a huge swig of the burning liquid, coughing hard as it hit the back of my throat.

"Good girl. Now let's get this party started!" She tottered out of the bedroom, pausing to spritz Calvin Klein, Obsession, liberally over the pair of us. "Come on, Simon's going to drive us." I followed her down the stairs and saw him waiting at the bottom, keys in hand. His eyes were wide as they travelled from my face, down my very exposed body and back up again. I wished I'd refused to give into Bonnie's hounding and worn my usual jeans and jumper combo. I met his shocked stare, wondering if he was about to go all dad like on me, like Handlebar had before. Would he send us both to get changed? Ban us from going entirely?

He said nothing, but his eyes didn't leave me as I made my way to the bottom of the stairs. I wrung my hands together, looking at the ground as Bonnie flapped around, grabbing our handbags, twirling for mum. "What do ya think?" Bonnie said, giving a little wiggle and prodding me in the side. "Come on, Is, give her a proper look." Mum stepped into the hallway, whisky in hand and I could see the tell-tail signs that she was already slipping. I'd been thinking it for days. Her eyes were not quite focused, her breath smelled like she'd been drinking for hours.

"You both look lovely. Beautiful," she nodded. Simon took the glass from her hand and for a second, I felt grateful. He would take care of her.

For once, I didn't have to worry – he would fix this. Still staring at me, he tipped the glass back, downing it in one go.

"Hey," Mum slurred. "That was mine."

"I'll get you another one."

She grinned, pushing him against the hallway wall, kissing him hard on the lips. I saw her tongue slip inside his mouth and looked away, but not before I saw his eyes, still trained on my face as he kissed her. Bonnie pushed between the pair of them without a trace of embarrassment. "Fuck off, Mum. We need him now."

"Oh, fine. But hurry back, okay?" She gave him a wink. "Have fun girls. Don't do anything I wouldn't do."

"Great advice, Mum," Bonnie laughed, kissing her on the cheek. She grabbed me by the hand before I could change my mind and pulled me out the door. Simon pulled it closed, following behind us as Bonnie ran ahead calling shotgun, and I felt the warm pressure of his hand on my lower back. He leaned close to my ear.

"You look beautiful, Belle. Be careful of boys tonight. They might try to take advantage of you, looking like that."

I smiled, grateful for his concern. "I'll be careful." I thought I felt his fingers graze the bare skin on my back, but then his hand was gone and he was climbing into the driver's seat. I took a breath and climbed into the car, hoping the night would go fast so I could get back to normal.

The room was spinning. Why the hell had I ever thought listening to Bonnie was a good idea? She'd talked me into drinking more. A lot more. There had been beer and then one of the older girls had passed round shots. I'd seen the look Bonnie gave me. The one that said don't you dare embarrass me.

Drink it. So I had. And now I was walking round a house full of strange people, weaving in and out of rooms I didn't recognise, trying to find my sister. I would kill her for this.

"Hey, baby!" A voice called and I turned around, squinting my eyes to focus. A boy with sandy blonde hair and blue eyes was grinning at me from the sofa. "Come and finish what you started!" He spread his legs and gave a suggestive wink.

"Eww. No."

He shrugged. "Your loss, Bonnie."

Yep. I would definitely kill her. I walked towards the stairs, half climbing, half crawling until I reached the top. "Bonnie!" I yelled. "Where are you?" I heard laughter and pushed open the door closest to me. Bonnie was lying on the bed, a year eleven boy from my class snogging the life out of her. Her dress was pushed up to her waist and my eyes opened wide as I saw the flex of his hand as his fingers pushed inside her, her thong pushed to one side. "Bonnie! What the hell?"

She broke away from his lips, turning her head lazily. "Oh, hi babe. Having fun?" I couldn't speak. The boy kept fingering her without missing a beat.

"I want to go. We're going home."

"Not yet..." she giggled as the boy whispered something against her throat. His hand paused as he looked up at me finally, and then his eyes bulged.

"Fuck, twins? Get in here."

Bonnie sighed. "You had to go and ruin it." She pushed his hand away from her crotch and stood up, yanking her dress back into place, and wriggling her bottom to straighten her underwear. "Oh well." She left him on the bed and walked over to me, taking my arm. "You're wasted."

"So are you," I slurred.

She laughed. "Yep." We leaned into each other as we stumbled down the stairs, falling into the wall and the banister. "He was gorgeous. I'm so jealous of you getting to take your classes with these guys. I'm stuck with the spotty pre-pubescent twats who only want to talk about bloody power rangers," she pouted.

"I'm there for the education. Not the boys."

"What a waste." She pushed open the front door. "What time is it?"

"No idea. The fresh air hit me like a blast of ice, making me feel even more drunk. "Bonnie... wait... I need to sit down."

"Oh go on then." She guided me to a low wall.

"Are we going to walk home? In these heels?"

"I guess." She slumped down beside me. "I feel sick."

"Mmm. Me too."

"You want a cigarette?"

"No. And you shouldn't either."

"Oh shut up." She pulled one from her little

shoulder bag and lit it, taking a deep drag as if to show me that I wasn't her boss. The smell made me want to vomit even more and I dipped my head between my legs, focusing on the gravel. We sat side by side, shivering on the wall, the backs of my thighs growing numb as they pressed into the bare brick. Footsteps approached and stopped in front of us and I glanced up, frowning in my attempt to focus.

"You girls look like you've had enough. You ready to go?"

"Simon!" I exclaimed, the word coming out more high pitched than I'd intended. "Did... did I call you?"

He gave a low chuckle. "No. But I guessed you might need a lift back."

"You were right." I tried to stand up, swayed and stumbled. He caught me against his chest.

"Oh dear... someone's had a bit too much to

drink."

"Never again..."

"Speak for yourself," Bonnie grinned, looking up at us. She held out a hand to Simon, but he didn't take it.

"Let's get you to the car, hey?" He wrapped an arm around my back and under my elbow, supporting me across the driveway and out to the road where he'd parked. He opened the door for me to climb inside, but I couldn't seem to make my feet work properly. "Here. Let me." He hoisted me into the passenger seat, leaning across me to buckle my seatbelt. I could smell the whisky on his breath and wondered if he should really be driving, but then my attention was caught by a squeal outside the car.

"She's fallen in the bush!" I giggled, pointing behind him to where Bonnie had landed on her back. She was flailing about like an upended tortoise in an attempt to get back up. Simon raised a disapproving eyebrow.

"She leads you astray. I don't like it."

"Oh, I'm not that easily led. Well, maybe tonight I was..." I giggled again. "Go and help her."

He sighed and nodded. I couldn't help but notice the way he grabbed her and heaved her into the car. There was none of the gentleness he'd had with me. Could it be that for once, I was the favourite? I felt awful to realise that I liked the notion. Bonnie had always been the one that was noticed, the one that shone. Was it so bad to feel good about being the favoured twin for a change? He left her to do her own seatbelt, which she ignored, lying out over the back seat and groaning.

"Don't be sick," he warned her, climbing into the driver's seat and firing up the engine. It was only a short drive home but the motion of the car made me feel even more wobbly and nauseous if that were possible. I knew Bonnie was faring no better by the groans coming from the back.

We finally made it home and Bonnie clambered out ungracefully, her dress up round her belly again. "Bonnie!" I whispered, mortified on her behalf. Simon looked over and shook his head, frowning.

"It's just bloody skin. Don't make a fuss," she slurred, making a half hearted attempt to pull it down. Simon took my arm, helping me forwards, my legs as heavy as lead.

"Your mum and Roxy are sleeping," he said in a low voice, "So no noise please." He opened the front door and Bonnie headed straight for the living room, flopping down belly first on the sofa, her eyes already closed. I wanted to go and pull her dress back into place, but I didn't think I could make it across the room without collapsing myself.

"Come here, you," Simon said softly. "Let's get you sorted." He guided me into the kitchen and I leaned heavily against the counter as the room span in circles. "Here." He took my hand, placing a glass of water into it. I felt it begin to slip and he held onto it, wrapping his hand over the top of mine. "Little sips. You're really going to feel this in the morning." I took a few small sips, feeling sicker with each one.

"No more," I shook my head.

"Okay. Maybe in a little while." He put the glass down, still holding onto my hand. It felt nice. Like he cared.

"Thank you," I mumbled. "For coming to get us. I didn't think we were going to make it back."

"You shouldn't put yourself in such dangerous positions. Did anyone try anything with you?"

"What do you mean?" I stared up at his face, trying to focus.

"Try to touch you?"

I thought of Bonnie, lying spread eagled on the bed with that boy's fingers thrusting inside her.

"No."

"Good. You're too pure to be ruined by those creeps."

I laughed, not understanding. He wrapped his arms around me, holding me to his chest. This was what it was like to have a dad. Someone to come and get you in the middle of the night, to care enough to make sure you were safe. Mum had put herself to bed without a second thought about her thirteen year old daughters, out drinking and doing god knows what. She didn't care. She hadn't for years.

"You're special, Isabel," he whispered into my hair. "Beautiful, clever Belle. You don't know how special you are." He kissed me on the forehead and I felt like I might burst with pride. He had noticed me. He thought I was special. Nobody else had ever said anything so wonderful to me before. The water had helped, I realised. I didn't feel so drunk now.

The room had stopped spinning. Simon had been right. I looked up at his face, seeing his eyes on mine as he leaned forward, kissing me on the forehead again. I felt as if a warm safe blanket had been placed over me.

"Thanks," I said, feeling shy at his praise. "I better go to bed now. I have loads of coursework to do tomorrow."

He nodded, not moving. I saw a question cross his face, like he was waiting for me to say something else. I didn't know what it could be. I felt silly and embarrassed, suddenly unsure if I had missed something important. Then, he smiled and leaned towards me. I tilted my head, sure that he was going to kiss me on the cheek and say goodnight as he had started doing lately. It was a sweet little ritual, one I had noticed he reserved just for me. But this time, he didn't kiss my cheek.

Instead, his lips pressed hard against mine. My

eyes widened in horror and surprise as I waited for him to pull away, but he didn't stop. He just kept moving his lips against mine, his hands coming up to the back of my neck, sliding beneath my hair. I felt his tongue slip inside my mouth, just as my mother had done to him earlier. The nausea returned instantly at the sensation. I'd never been kissed by a boy before, but I knew enough to know that this was wrong. His body pressed into mine, pinning me to the counter and I was disgusted to see his eyes sink closed as if he were lost in the pleasure of the moment. This was all wrong. He was ruining everything! This wasn't supposed to be happening.

With a desperate need to stop him, I shoved him hard in the chest, hearing the gasp as he fell back. "No," I said, my voice quivering. "No." I couldn't look at him, I just ran as fast as I could up the stairs, slamming my bedroom door behind me. He didn't follow.

Chapter Twenty-Five

1990

The room was painfully bright as I struggled with the monumental task of opening my eyes. I'd fallen asleep without pulling the curtains closed, and now I could see the sun was high and bright. I'd slept away half my precious Saturday, when I should have been working on my English essay. My lips were dry, my tongue stuck gluily to the roof of my mouth and with a shiver, I realised I'd never made it out of the green dress, nor under the quilt. I pulled myself up to a sitting position, wrapping my arms round my bare knees. Bonnie wasn't there. We'd shared the lumpy double bed for as long as I could remember, and waking up without her there was a strange experience. I was always the first to rise. I guessed she must have stayed on the sofa, right where she'd fallen, but knowing her, she would be faring far better than I was. She was probably swigging black coffee and laughing about the party already.

I rubbed my eyes, trying to piece together the fuzzy images in my mind. One was brighter than the rest. Simon had kissed me, and not in a dad way. He'd snogged me. I didn't have the first idea what I was going to do about it. If I told mum, I was almost certain I would get the blame for leading him on. I knew she liked him more than the previous boyfriends and she wasn't exactly the type you could go to with serious stuff like this. Even if she did take my side, it would likely throw her over the edge. I knew it was only a matter of time before she ended up sectioned again, and I wasn't ready to lose her yet. So mum was not an option.

Roxy was completely wrapped up in her own social life, not to mention her school work, and she was barely home. I knew she tried to avoid mum as much as possible. I couldn't blame her, it was painful to witness. If I told her though, if I shared what had happened, I knew she wouldn't ignore me. She would listen. But it wouldn't make any difference. Mum would still take his side and it would end up as a massive scene. I wasn't a baby anymore. I didn't need to run to my big sister. I would deal with it myself, just pretend it hadn't happened. He'd been drinking anyway, the taste of the whisky on his lips had been strong. Maybe he was just as humiliated as I was now. I didn't want an apology. I just wanted to move on and put it firmly in the past.

I crept out into the hallway, hearing sounds of movement from downstairs as I went into the bathroom. I turned the shower hotter than I usually liked it, washing away the stale smell of alcohol, letting the steam cleanse my pores. It helped. Dressing in my favourite baggy dungarees with a cosy fleece jumper over the top, I finally summoned the courage to go downstairs and face everyone.

"Good morning, sleepy head," Mum laughed as I came into the kitchen. I frowned, surprised at her warm tone.

"You okay, Mum?" I asked. I saw Simon give a tiny shake of his head over her shoulder, and felt relieved that mum had provided an opportunity for us to break the ice.

"I'm fine. Absolutely fine. We're having a party!"

"No, we're not," Simon said firmly.

"Yes, we fucking are." She leaned forward and my stomach sank as I saw what she was doing.

"Simon! Stop her!"

"Believe me, I've tried." He shook his head as

she snorted a long line of white powder from the kitchen side. She looked up, her nose red, her eyes wild.

"You're a bunch of boring losers. Come and find me when you're ready to have some real fun!" She stormed towards the front door and rattled it furiously.

"I've hidden the key," Simon murmured. "I'm sorry but I don't know where she'll end up in this state if she goes out by herself."

I nodded, watching sadly. Mum kicked the door with a final scream and then stormed upstairs, defeated. A moment later we heard the deafening sound of dance music coming from her room.

"And I thought I was supposed to be the teenager," I said softly.

"I'm sorry you had to see that."

"Where's Bon?" I asked, clasping my hands together nervously. I didn't want to be alone with him. That easy atmosphere between us had disappeared and now I felt awkward.

"Living room."

"Oh. Okay. I'll just..." I pointed behind me and he nodded, his eyes on mine. I pushed open the door to the living room, surprised to find her curled up in the big armchair, dressed in a tracksuit, a blanket pulled tightly around her body. She was staring blankly at the television, though I saw her shoulders tense as I came in. Was she angry at me for making her leave last night? "You okay, Bon Bon?" I smiled. "I hate to say it but you look worse than me!"

"Funny."

"You hungover?"

"Something like that."

"But you had fun though?"

"Did you?"

I shrugged. "I don't think I'm ready for those

kind of parties to be honest with you. I'll probably wait a few more years."

"I bet."

"What's that supposed to mean?" I frowned as I perched on the arm of her chair. "I said I'd give it a try and I did. I just didn't really enjoy it. But you seemed to."

She shrugged, still staring at the TV screen. I glanced at the door, sure that Simon wouldn't be able to hear me over the racket of Mum's music. "Hey," I whispered. "Something happened last night."

Bonnie straightened, her eyes on mine. "Tell me."

"When we got back here... in the kitchen."

"What?" Her voice was urgent and I felt silly bringing it up.

I took a breath. "He... Simon... he kissed me. With tongues." I felt my face flame as I whispered the words. Bonnie stared at me, her eyes hardening and instantly I knew I'd made a mistake in telling her.

"He *kissed* you?"

I nodded.

"And you're oh so traumatised by the big bad tongue, is that it?"

"I – Bonnie! You know I've never done that before, not with anyone. I would have told you."

"Oh just grow up will you, Isabel! Nobody cares."

I felt the tears well up in my eyes. Bonnie was never like this, not with me. She'd always been the one person I could share anything with. Why was she being so horrible? The door opened and Simon walked in carrying a tray with three mugs of tea, along with a packet of paracetamol.

"Thought you might need this," he said, setting the tray down with a cautious smile. He was trying to make amends. And maybe he wouldn't bring up the kiss. Maybe we could forget it ever happened. I wiped my eyes, plastering on a smile.

"Thanks." I picked up a mug and passed it to Bonnie who shook her head.

"I don't want it."

"You feeling sick?"

"Very." She looked down at her lap.

"I'm not surprised," Simon smirked. "You were out of control last night, Bonnie."

"What?" she asked, her voice cold as she stared at him. I had never seen her look at anyone with such hatred before.

"You were wasted and flaunting yourself like a piece of meat." He looked at me, his eyes softening. "Some people are special, they have some class. And some," he looked at Bonnie, "Just give it out on a plate."

"Simon!" I gasped, horrified.

Bonnie jumped to her feet and I curled into myself, knowing what was coming. I'd seen it a thousand times before, the way she exploded when challenged by one of mum's boyfriends. She had never figured out the art of self restraint. She was brutally honest and it was always frightening, yet thoroughly entertaining to watch. But she didn't let him have it. She didn't shout or swear or do any of the usual Bonnie things. Instead, she burst into tears and ran from the room. It was the most shocking thing she could have done, something I'd never seen before.

"What was that about?" I whispered, looking at the door she'd slammed behind her.

"I'm sorry." I looked up, trying to figure out if he meant for upsetting my sister or for last night. He held my gaze. "I just don't like the way she acts. She doesn't value herself. She's bad for you."

"She's my sister." I placed the tea on the table.

"How can she be bad for me?" I didn't wait for him to answer.

Bonnie was curled on the bed, her back towards the door, the duvet half pulled over her. "Hey," I said softly, coming into the room and closing the door. "You okay?" She didn't answer. "Bonnie?"

"I'm fine," she spat, not turning to face me. "Just leave me alone."

"Bon..."

"I mean it, Issy. I don't want to talk. Not to you."

Her words were like a wrecking ball. "Not to me?" I repeated. "But – "

"But nothing, okay? Just get out. I don't want to look at you."

I stood frozen in the doorway. It had been her who'd insisted we go out to the party. Her who'd decided we should do shots, and her who'd gone off with that boy and let him in her pants when I doubted she even knew his name. I bet Simon had said something to her about acting like a slut and now she'd got her back up because she was jealous that he thought I was the special one instead of her. Trust her to lose her mind over being second best. But she was being a bitch. I'd told her about the kiss in the hopes that she'd have some advice for me, after all, Simon was right – she did have plenty of experience in that department. I'd wanted her help. But now, sick as the idea was, I was certain she was jealous of that too. He'd kissed me rather than her and she couldn't stand it.

"Fine," I said coldly. "Sulk all you want."

I closed the door and went into the hall feeling the anger pulsing through me. I pushed open Roxy's door, but she wasn't there. Out with her friends, I supposed. Finally I pushed open mum's bedroom door. The constant deafening thump of the music was making my head ache and I wanted to ask her to turn it down. "Mum?" I said, stepping into her room. She was by the window, pacing back and forth, her lips moving fast as though she were muttering something, though she wasn't making a sound. I moved to the stereo, turning the music down. When she didn't look round, I shrugged to myself and switched it off completely. She continued to pace, her hands clasped in front of her, her left thumbnail rubbing harsh lines into the back of her right hand. "Mum?" I said again. Nothing. I swallowed and pulled open her bedside cabinet drawer. "Have you taken your pills today?" I asked, picking up the packet and running my finger over the foil. "Here," I popped one out and held it towards her. She didn't respond, she just continued to mutter to herself.

It was no good. I had to talk to Simon. I had to tell him that we needed to take mum in to see the doctor. I put the pill gently on the bedside cabinet and backed away. "It will be okay, Mum. We'll fix this." She didn't look up. Didn't even register that I was in the room with her. Not for the first time I wished that I had someone else for a mother. Someone who could take care of me, rather than the other way round.

"Mum needs help," I said, coming back into the living room where Simon sat on the sofa.

"I know. It's in hand."

"Really?"

"Come. Sit." He nodded to the place beside him on the sofa and I hesitated. Could I trust him? But then I saw the flash of hurt that crossed his face and realised he was just as humiliated as I was. I had to give him a chance to put this right, to get back to how we had been before he messed up. I moved to sit down beside him and he took my hand. I forced myself not to flinch away. "Your mum isn't well."

"I know. It's not like it's the first time."

"This has happened before?"

"Yes. A lot. She's had Bipolar since I was eight."

He nodded, his expression unreadable. "I'll deal with it."

"You will?"

"Yes. I'll see to it."

I didn't know what that meant but I was too drained to ask. I was just relieved that this time, it wouldn't be up to me and Roxy. We could leave it to the grown ups for once. "Thanks Simon." I made to get back up but his grasp on my hand tightened.

"Wait." He took a breath. "About last night."

"Simon, don't. Let's just forget it ever happened, please?"

"I can't do that."

"What? Why?"

"Belle." He scooted across the cushion so his thigh was touching mine. I wanted to pull away but

I didn't want to hurt his feelings, not after he'd promised to take care of mum. "Look at me. You and I have something. Something special. I felt it the first time your mum showed me your picture, and then when we met, I knew I wasn't imagining it. There's something between us. You're special. I know I keep saying it, but it's true. You're not like other women."

"I'm not a woman. I'm thirteen."

"You're more mature than any woman I've ever met."

"So? I'm still thirteen."

"Belle. You don't have to be shy with me."

"I'm not being shy." I felt my eyes fill with tears and looked down at my knees, wishing everything could go back to how it had been. "I'm just sad. I thought you would be like a dad to me. That's what I wanted. I *needed* you to be a dad, and you're ruining it."

He shook his head. "For Christ sake, I don't want to be your fucking dad. I want *you!* Can't you see, it's the entire reason I'm here? For you Belle!"

I yanked my hand out of his and jumped to my feet, tears streaming down my cheeks. "Well I don't want you! This is wrong, can't you see that? You were supposed to be my dad. Not my boyfriend!" I shouted, not caring if mum heard me.

He shook his head, rubbing a palm across his chin and taking a deep breath. He looked up at me, his eyes softening. "You aren't ready. I'm sorry. I rushed in too fast. But you will be, Belle. And I can wait."

"I won't ever want this. Not ever."

"I can wait."

"Don't," I whispered, feeling sick to my stomach. "Please, just don't."

Chapter Twenty-Six

I stood, unmoving in the kitchen, the offending box laid out on the table in front of me, the necklace glinting from it's bed of velvet, where I'd dropped it, taunting me. I didn't want to touch it again, to have the feel of the cold metal brush against my skin. I wanted to bury it, grab a hammer and smash it into a thousand pieces. The phone rang and I jumped, my breath catching as I instinctively picked up the handset so the noise didn't wake Sophie. Slowly I brought it to my ear, too frightened to be the first to speak.

"Issy?" came Lucas's deep, soothing voice. "You there?"

"Yes..." I breathed, "Yes, sorry, I'm here. Hi."

"Hi." He paused. "Um, I thought you might

come back tonight... you said you felt scared at home and I hoped we could talk... about what happened."

"You're regretting it," I said, my voice flat. I had known this was coming.

"Actually, no. I'm not. Are you?"

I sighed. "Yes... No. Oh, I don't know, Lucas. I feel confused and guilty and part of me wishes we hadn't crossed that line. But it's done now, isn't it?"

"Come over. You can stay again and we'll talk about this."

"I can't. It's late. Sophie's already in bed."

"I'll come to you then. Oscar's out at a sleepover."

"No... not tonight Lucas. I – I have some things I need to figure out."

There was a beat of silence and then he spoke. "Okay. Not tonight then. But Issy, you can't let guilt over how Roxy may or may not have felt, stop you from doing something that might make you happy. I meant what I said. There's been something between us for a while now, you and I both know that and I don't see why we shouldn't go there."

I nodded into the phone. "I need some time. I need to think about it."

"Take all the time you want. I'm not going anywhere. Are you going to be okay tonight? You won't be frightened?"

I bit my lip, looking across to the necklace on the kitchen counter. "I'll be fine."

"Okay. Goodnight Issy."

"Night Lucas."

I hung up the phone and with a fierce surge of determination I reached forward and picked up the necklace, feeling the lightness of it in my palm. I had lied to Lucas. I didn't need time to think about my feelings for him. I wanted him, and I'd known it for the past eighteen months. We'd always been close, but somehow time had changed our relationship and I'd begun to feel a spark when I'd looked into his eyes. I'd known that he cared for me, I just hadn't realised he felt something more than a platonic love between us until last night. But that kiss had been anything but platonic.

I would have liked nothing more than to go to him now, curl up in his arms and be happy for once, but I couldn't do that. Not while so much needed to be cleared up. I couldn't keep running from my fears, being controlled by my past and by the actions of one bad man. I ran the delicate chain through my fingers and placed it back in its box, snapping it closed. My hand slipped inside my pocket, closing around the knife as I went to the front door, sliding back the bolt and opening it wide. With a steadying breath, I stepped out onto the porch. The world was dark and quiet. I waited, expecting to see a shadow loom from behind the bushes, a deep, knowing voice congratulating me on making the right choice, but nobody came.

"I know you're out there," I said softly. My heart pounded frantically in my chest, but I kept my stance strong, refusing to look weak as I challenged the darkness. "Come out," I demanded, my voice hard, though I didn't dare shout in case the neighbours came to investigate. I waited, my fingers sweating around the knife, the sound of the breeze disturbing the leaves in Ted's sycamore tree. A car came round the corner, headlights blaring and I jumped, bracing myself, but it didn't slow. It drove past, the driver not even glancing in my direction. "Where are you?" I murmured under my breath, surprised and unsettled. I'd been so sure he'd be waiting. That he would come. But of course, he wouldn't want me to have the upper hand, to be the one in control. He'd wait until he had the chance to catch me off guard. I stared blindly into the darkness, seeing nothing out of place, and then, feeling deflated, my chance to be brave stolen from under me, I turned and went back indoors, turning the key in the lock behind me.

Chapter Twenty-Seven

1990

I felt like I was losing control of everything. Ever since the night of the party, it seemed as though I had been dragged down a path I didn't want to be on, but as hard as I fought against it, I couldn't seem to find a way back. Mum had stopped talking to all of us, refusing to communicate with anyone except Simon. I was sure he was whispering in her ear, playing on her paranoia, because she had become certain he was the only person she could trust. He promised it wasn't the case and that he was in talks with her doctors, but I had never seen her turn against us so fiercely before. It hurt more than I wanted to admit.

Bonnie, my best friend in the world and the one person who had helped me through all the shit with mum in the past, was still being cold and abrupt with me. She'd been going to bed early, pretending to be asleep so we couldn't chat when I came up. And now I couldn't even talk to Simon because I knew his true feelings. He'd made it clear that he wasn't interested in playing the role of my father – he wanted me to be his girlfriend. It was completely sick and I felt more lonely than I ever had in my life.

I leaned over the small desk in my room, trying to concentrate on my maths coursework, and failing spectacularly. Roxy had taken mum out for some fresh air on Simon's instruction and Bonnie had been out at a sleepover and was yet to return. There was no way I was going to sit downstairs with Simon, so I'd shut myself off in my room and was grateful that at least he hadn't followed me up.

I heard the front door bang and wondered if Bonnie was finally back. I hoped she'd be in a better mood after a night out. Maybe we could finally get back to being friendly. Abandoning my coursework, I walked out to the landing. I could hear voices coming from the living room so I padded down the stairs, my feet bare. The door was closed, and I was just about to push it open when I heard Bonnie cry out. I put my ear to the door, listening hard.

"Get off, I mean it."

"Oh don't act like you haven't been out giving it away to everyone else."

"Simon, please!"

"Shut up. You know I hate you saying my name. You don't get to do that." I heard the unmistakable sound of skin meeting skin and wondered in shock if he'd slapped her. "You'll give it to me, you little bitch. And if you don't, I'll go and take what I really want. Would you really do that to her?"

"You wouldn't touch Isabel. You and I both know that. What was it you said? She's too pure for you to ruin but I'm soiled goods so it doesn't matter?"

"I'm glad you know your place. Now shut up and open your fucking legs."

"No!"

There was another slap, the sound of a zipper opening and then Simon groaned. Bonnie was completely silent. Why wasn't she fighting? I stood rooted to the ground, a lump in my throat that threatened to choke me. I had to go in, I had to stop him. But what could I do? What if he turned on me? What if he refused to help mum? My hand shook, hovering just above the door handle, and then slowly, I pulled it away, turning and padding silently back up to my room. I put my headphones in my ears and turned the music up loud.

Keep It Secret

A little while later, I heard the shower running. The sound continued for almost an hour, until eventually, Bonnie came into the bedroom wrapped in a towel, her eyes puffy, her hair dripping down her back. I looked up from where I was pretending to read a novel on the bed. "Hey." She mumbled something in reply, but I didn't catch it. "How was the sleepover?"

"Fine."

"Many people there?"

"A few. Why do you care?"

"I'm just trying to make conversation." I felt sick with tension, the elephant sitting in the room, blocking the transparency we'd always had between us. I wanted to ask her if she was okay. If Simon had done what I thought he'd done, but then she would know that I had heard. That I had let it happen. I was a fucking coward and I knew it. "Bonnie..."

"What?"

"Have you..." I didn't know how to ask, to be there for her. "Uh, have you got a hangover? I have some paracetamol in the drawer if you want some?" I said, grasping for words to fill the tense silence.

Bonnie glared at me, her eyes red and bloodshot. "Oh, of course, because why wouldn't I have a hangover, right? Knowing me I just spent a night doing shots and sucking dicks, because that's all I'm good for, isn't it?"

"I didn't mean – "

"Oh I know exactly what you meant. Keep your fucking paracetamol, I don't want anything from you. Why don't you just get back to your clever little piece of coursework and keep proving how you're better than everyone else. I wouldn't want to disturb precious little Issy, would I?"

"Bonnie!"

She pulled on a pair of jeans and a hoodie, her

long red hair still dripping, soaking through the cotton. "Fuck you, Is. I don't need your sympathy." She walked out slamming the bedroom door shut behind her. A second later, the front door slammed shut. She was gone.

Bonnie hadn't come home for three days and nobody seemed to care. I'd called everyone we knew from school, but nobody would admit to having seen her, and mum and Simon refused to call the police. They were drinking JD and coke in the kitchen, and mum was dancing to Bob Marley like she didn't have a care in the world. Roxy had gone on a school trip to Paris for the week and I'd never felt more alone. "She'll come back, she's a big girl," Simon said, trying to drape an arm round my shoulder. I squirmed away, disgusted at the brush of his skin against mine.

"This is your fault," I whispered through gritted

teeth.

He raised an eyebrow. "How so?"

"You know."

He stared at me, comprehension dawning on his face. "Oh." He shrugged. "Is that my fault? Or is it yours, Belle?"

"What?"

"I told you I'd be patient. I didn't say I'd be abstinent. And she's the closest I could get to the real thing. What else did you expect me to do?"

My mouth dropped open at his audacity. I couldn't believe he was admitting it so freely, my mother in the same room. He knew the power he held over her, over all of us. "You're disgusting."

"I disagree. But we said we wouldn't discuss this until you were ready. You're still so innocent, lovely girl. You don't understand these things. Not like your sister."

"Don't touch her again. I mean it."

He leaned forward and I flinched at the smell of his skin. His aftershave, a smell I had once associated with comfort now repulsed me. "Does this mean you've changed your mind? You want to take her place? Because you know she's nothing but a stand in. It's *you* I want, you don't have to be jealous." He ran a finger down my collarbone, and I slapped his hand away. I glanced at mum, wanting her to pay attention. To do something. She was sloshing neat whisky into her glass. Her eyes met mine briefly and then she downed it in one, and walked out, leaving me alone with him.

"I want you to leave, Simon. We don't want you here."

"I'll leave. When you say you'll come with me." I shook my head and he pursed his lips. "Then don't complain about what goes on between me and your sister. You can't have it both ways, sweetheart." He followed mum out of the kitchen and I stared after him. An hour later, Bonnie came home.

The door creaked slowly open, the glow of the hall light seeping through my tightly closed eyelids. The tick tick tick of the grandfather clock echoed through the silent house, the only sound besides the panicked thumping of my heart pounding in my ears as I held my breath. I counted to five, my thoughts rushing from one to the next, escape plans popping into my mind before evaporating like the drying tears on a baby's round cheek. Then, just as I knew it would, a heavy footstep broke past the threshold of the room, destroying any illusion of sanctuary. I had known it would come to this. I could picture exactly what he looked like, though I didn't open my eyes, not even a flicker. The shoes, shiny, fashionable loafers he wore to the office, grew closer, bringing with them the smell of whisky, almost overpowering in its intensity.

I could hear the uneven, heavy breathing now, could imagine the rancid smell of his breath, the onion we'd eaten for dinner, mixed with cigarettes and alcohol. The footsteps paused and I knew he had reached the foot of the bed. I kept perfectly still, forcing myself to breath, to feign sleep. He could not know that I was awake. A sound broke through the silence, the jingle of keys clattering to the floorboards, and a sharp intake of breath as he froze, waiting. I crossed my fingers tightly, hidden beneath the blankets as I waited too, desperately hoping to hear the sound of my mother rousing, to come and see what he was doing, to stop him once and for all.

The silence continued, undisturbed, save for the tick tick ticking of the clock. I heard him let out the breath and then, the mattress sagged as he climbed onto it, sliding along it like the poisonous viper I knew he was. I kept silent. If I couldn't see him, it couldn't be happening. I could make it into a dream, a nightmare brought on by watching too many episodes of Buffy the vampire slayer. It wasn't real. My mouth filled with hot saliva as the smell of his aftershave hit my nostrils, but I didn't dare to swallow it down. He would see. He would know I was awake.

I heard the slide of his buckle and felt my body tilt involuntarily on the mattress as he positioned himself, lowering himself down. There was a grunt and a gasp, and then the hot, deceitful tears began to slide down my cheeks. But still, I kept my eyes closed. Pretended I didn't know. Because if I was asleep, if I didn't know, I couldn't be to blame for not stopping him.

Chapter Twenty-Eight

The irony had never escaped me that I'd chosen to raise Sophie without any attempt to find a father figure for her, when I'd spent my entire life wishing for one of my own. Being fatherless had shaped the person I'd become, affected every single aspect of my life. Some people say it's easier when they die, rather than just walk out on you, but I disagree. At least if they leave, there's a chance they may come back. There's hope. I never had that. Not ever.

I don't remember the man who created me at all. The man who died of cancer when I was just two years old. There were pictures of him around the house when we were growing up, a stocky, smiley man with thick dark hair and dark, sparkling eyes, just like Roxy. In some of the photos he'd had a moustache, and I had often imagined watching him trim it, my legs swinging over the side of the bath as he combed it over the sink. I made up all sorts of painfully normal scenarios I might have found him in; Cutting the grass with our rickety old petrol lawnmower while I used my little pink watering can to water the borders. He would have smiled and told me I was helpful, he was proud of me. Or stroking my hair, just like I'd seen Lacey's dad do when she'd cut open her knee playing kiss chase. I hadn't been able to tear my eyes from them as he told her he wasn't ready for her to start kissing boys yet, a protective arm wrapping around her shoulder as he shook his head, grinning at the other mums at the school gate. I wanted a dad to care about me, to kiss my scrapes better. I wanted to know I mattered too.

Roxy had once told me that before she got ill, mum would talk about dad all the time. That she was forever telling us stories about what a great man he was, kind, funny, intelligent – but I can't recall a single one. I can't remember a time when she wasn't ill, and that hurt, because I knew I was being unfair to her. She was a good mum for a long time, or so I'd been told. I just didn't remember.

Not knowing about my dad became something I'd come to accept at some point. I never found out what his favourite colour was, or if he hated ice cream, like me, or how he liked to spend his free time. I didn't even know what he had done for work, aside from that he had been into investments. He'd left us a lot of money when he'd died, and I supposed that was at least some small blessing. It had meant we didn't lose everything when mum started going in and out of hospital. It had also meant that we could move house without worrying about how to afford it.

When, at sixteen, Roxy had declared she intended to get into Oxford university, mum, in a rare moment of sanity, had packed up and relocated us from Bath to Oxford without hesitation. She'd also insisted on changing our surnames from Michaels to Cormack, a move that both Bonnie and I understood completely, though we never spoke of it. It had been the one thing she'd ever done to show she cared. She understood what she'd put us through and I'd realised then that she'd seen more than she'd ever let on. She knew what Simon had done. The fact that she'd let it happen would be something I could never forgive, but in taking us away, giving us fresh new identities, she was at least trying to break his hold over us.

Roxy had been furious about changing her surname, ranting about letting dad go, disrespecting him, but she'd been so aware of mum's fragile mental health and so grateful to her for deciding to move to Oxford that she'd backed down eventually. I never did find out what mum had told her to convince her, but I was certain Roxy never knew our secret. I would have seen the pity in her eyes.

We'd all hoped that the move, the beautiful new house, as yet untainted by our history, the fresh, exciting start would be exactly what mum needed to find her way back. To heal from her mental health troubles at last. But it wasn't to be.

If anything, things became worse. Perhaps it was her guilt at all the things she'd turned a blind eye to. No matter how good a mother she might once have been, there was no way she could claim that now. Not after all we'd lived through. I will never know what pushed her to breaking point, but whatever it was, mum began craving oblivion on a scale we'd never seen before. She refused point blank to take her pills, and though I knew it was happening, she begged me never to tell the others – a promise I kept. I loved her, but I hated her too. I was drowning in confusion, isolated and scared and angry. And I was so wrapped up in my own guilt, the idea that Simon had considered me too special to hurt, so had taken what he wanted from Bonnie, using her to fulfil his sick needs, mum not taking her pills had seemed like such a minor issue all things considered. I was wrong, of course. Less than two years after moving into the Oxford house, she hung herself. I have never stopped blaming myself for that. I know my sisters blamed me too when they found out my secret.

Even as an adult, I often wondered who I would be if I'd had two, healthy, normal parents to guide me through life. What I could have done if I hadn't had to grow up without a parent I could lean on. If I'd still make the same choices. I liked to think my childhood was to blame for my bad decisions, the actions I'd taken in anger and fear, but part of me knew, it was just who I was. There are some things you can't change, no matter how hard you try.

Keep It Secret

I sat bolt upright in bed, dragged from a nightmare, my hair plastered to my cheek with sweat and tears. I'd kicked the cover off the bed and was shivering, dressed only in the thin cotton Victorian style nightgown I loved to sleep in. I picked up my phone, pressing the button to illuminate the screen so I could check the time. Midnight. Damn. Still a long time to wait until the reassuring light of the new dawn crept over the horizon. I was just moving to pull the quilt back onto the bed when I heard it. Soft, but undeniable. Music. Coming from downstairs. Was Sophie out of bed? She'd once got up to watch TV in the middle of the night, having never been allowed to have cartoons in her first home. Actually, I might have left the TV on, I thought hazily, as I clambered off the mattress and headed for the stairs. I'd stayed up watching a film, trying to distract myself from thoughts of who might be lurking nearby. I must have left it on as I'd stumbled up to my bed, desperate for sleep.

I ran down the stairs, taking them two at a time, eager to return to my warm duvet as quickly as possible. Pushing open the living room door, I froze, the music no longer muffled as it tinkled out, engulfing me. It was jazz, soft saxophone, the kind that gave me chills from the memories it brought back. I gasped at the scene that greeted me. The room was filled with burning candles, on the tables, the mantelpiece, the hearth, all flickering, casting a soft, romantic glow over the room. And there, reclined on my sofa with a relaxed expression on his face, a glass of whisky in his hand, was Simon. I stared at him, realising how stupid I had been to walk in with nothing. My eyes flickered down to my body, knowing he'd be drinking in the sight of me. I wrapped my arms tightly around myself, trying to cover my chest, silently cursing my stupidity for not picking up the knife which remained uselessly in my trouser pocket, slung over my dresser chair upstairs.

My thoughts flew to Sophie. Could I reach her before he got to me? There was no lock on her door for us to barricade ourselves in. And my mobile phone was in my room, on the bedside cabinet. It was no good trapping ourselves with no way of calling for help. I didn't want him getting anywhere near my daughter. I couldn't lead him upstairs. Could I get to the land-line in the kitchen in time? Maybe, but I would never get through to anyone before he caught up to me. I would have to be clever here. I *was* clever. I had to remember that. Not fall victim to the fear. Easier said than done.

Simon smiled at me. "You've grown up, Belle. It's been a long time." He lifted his glass toward me, offering up a toast before taking a sip.

I stared at him, seeing the changes in his own face. He was still a handsome man, even now. Clean shaven, dark, almost black hair, that looked too perfect to be natural. He probably dyed it, I realised. There wasn't a grey hair on his head. His suit looked expensive, and his body had filled out which was unsettling. Not fat. Muscular. He had always seemed tall to me, but where I'd hoped that age might have diminished him, made him seem weaker, the reality was he looked more powerful than ever, even if he was approaching fifty. He saw my eyes travel over his frame and smiled, leaning forward. There were wrinkles around his eyes, but also deep lines around his mouth that looked hard and unforgiving. "I can see you've missed me too."

I ignored his comment. "Why are you here, Simon?"

"For you. You know that."

"I haven't seen you in twenty-two years. Why

now?"

He tilted his head, his eyes soft, though I wouldn't fall into the trap of trusting them. "I never stopped looking for you, you know. You must have know I'd come, after you were all over the TV? You couldn't have believed that I wouldn't see."

"Whatever happened in our past, it's over Simon. There was never anything between us, and there still won't be now. I want you to leave."

"No. You don't want that. I know you don't." He drained his glass and got to his feet. Took a step towards me. And another. Panic coursed through me. I turned, running for the kitchen, knowing he was following fast. I grabbed a knife from the block on the side, a flash of deja vu washing over me as I realised I had chosen the very knife I'd bought only last week, to replace the one the police had taken as evidence after I'd stabbed David. I spun, my back against the sink, holding the knife out in front of me.

"Don't you fucking come any closer. I'm not joking, Simon, I'll do it."

"Oh, I don't doubt that. You're surprisingly feisty for such a sweet girl."

"I'm not a *girl*. Though I'm sure you wish I was. That's what you like, isn't it Simon? Girls. Children!"

He raised an eyebrow. "Don't do that. You're twisting the truth."

"Am I? In what way?"

"Belle, come on. You're being unfair. Making out like I'm some dirty old predator that goes after kids." I stared at him blankly. That was exactly who he was. He pursed his lips. "I wasn't that much older than you, was I? Hardly over a decade. It's nothing."

"It's not nothing when you were twenty-five and Bonnie and I were only thirteen, Simon. It's a hell of a jump."

"I am not a predator. I'm a man who fell in love. You know how I felt about you. I can't help that you weren't the right age in the eyes of the law. Who makes these arbitrary rules up anyway? Who decides what's too big an age gap?"

"Me. *I* am telling you. Like I told you then. It was wrong. And you knew it too. You can pretend all you like, but you knew it."

"I knew people wouldn't understand. People don't understand a lot of things, with their small little minds, their black and white rules. They aren't like us, Belle. They can't think abstractly. They don't have the intelligence to step outside their comfortable rules and challenge the status quo."

"So they're wrong and you're right. You're just too clever for normal conventions, is that it? Can't squeeze your worldly mind into their tight little boxes."

"I never hurt you," he said softly. He looked hurt, pained at the idea. He never did understand. "I would never hurt you, you know that."

"You did. Don't you get it, Simon? You hurt Bonnie, and that was worse than if you'd done it to me. You tore out my heart the moment you laid a finger on her."

"Bonnie was always going to go down a bad path. If it hadn't been me, it would have just as easily been someone else. She was a wreck of a girl. She was never like you."

His words ignited a fury inside me, questions that had burned unanswered for years coming to the surface now. I couldn't hold back my rage as I held the knife in his direction, the blade shaking. "Why was it always her though? You never touched me, not once!"

"You were jealous," he said, smirking.

"Don't you dare. You think I'm angry because I

wanted you for myself? You sick bastard! I never wanted you. Don't ever make that assumption, because you're wrong. So wrong. But if it had been both of us, we'd have been in it together. We could have survived what you did. You didn't care about that though, did you? You didn't care that you broke us."

"Belle." His voice was a warning but I couldn't let him stop me. Not when I'd waited the last twenty-two years to let it all out. To tell him how much I hated him.

"You forced me to listen, to lay there night after night as you raped her, with no way of stopping you! I had to live with that guilt, knowing I should have done something. We could have stopped you if we'd worked together, but I never tried and I hate myself for that. You ruined everything. Why did you have to do that to her and not me?"

"I couldn't do that to you, Belle. You know

why."

"I don't."

"Yes. You do. Bonnie was a slut. You do know she wasn't even a virgin the first time I fucked her. She didn't even bleed."

"Shut up! I don't want to hear your sick lies! She was thirteen years old. Even if she had been with someone, it would have been a boy. One of the guys from school. You were a man. A sick, fucked up man and you took advantage of her."

"Don't you tell me to shut up, Belle," he said coldly. "You asked and now I'm going to give you an answer. You were fully aware of how I felt about you. From the first moment your mum showed me your picture, I knew I had to meet you. You were beautiful and clever and strong and I loved you. And I *wanted* you. I still do. I always will." He made to come closer to me and I thrust the knife in his direction. Standing in a kitchen, brandishing a knife at a dangerous man was a nightmare I seemed to be destined to re-live over and over again. It was hard to believe only three weeks had passed since I'd killed someone in this very room. I was being forced to do things I never should have been capable of. Never *would* have been capable of if these men would just leave me alone.

"Stay back! I mean it, Simon!"

He held out his hands, flashing me a smile. "Anything you ask, my sweet Belle. You know that." I flinched and he continued speaking, his voice bringing back so many memories I wished I could erase. "You know how hard it was for me, living with you and never laying a hand on you. I wanted you more than I could stand. It made me crazy, Belle. It felt like my skin was too tight, like I was on fire. I've never needed anything as much as I needed you. But I respected you too much to do that to you. You weren't ready. I was willing to wait.

But Bonnie, well, she was there for the taking, wasn't she? She never fought. Not after the first time, at least," he said. "And if she kept quiet, I could almost pretend she was you. She was never as beautiful though," he sniffed, as though a bad smell had crossed his path. "There was a hardness to her features that you never had. She never had your innocence, she was already tainted, long before I laid a hand on her. That's why I knew it wouldn't matter."

"You're disgusting. Of course it mattered. Do you have any idea of the damage you caused? The nightmare she's been through with her mental health? You pushed her over the edge."

He gave a careless shrug, his eyes trained on mine, unwavering in their intensity. "I used to watch your face while I fucked her, you know. You always kept your eyes shut, didn't you?" He touched his index and middle fingertips to his bottom lip, running them slowly over it as if he were imagining the pressure of a kiss. He breathed deep, silent for a moment, then gave a low laugh. "Sweet, innocent little thing that you were. I knew you were awake, listening, wanting it for yourself. Wishing it was you I was sliding into. I couldn't wait for the time to come when you'd tell me you were ready. I knew how jealous I was making you, but it wasn't our time yet. We both had to be patient, didn't we my love?"

He frowned, his hand moving to his chin as he rubbed the clean shaven skin of his jaw. "I always worried I'd push you too far one day. And I was right." His hands moved to the bottom of his crisp white shirt, fingers working to untuck it from his trousers, and he pulled it up, revealing his pale, taught abdomen. He pulled it higher and I saw the thick, puckered scar running horizontally down his breastbone, faded to pink after two decades of healing.

He watched my face, my eyes riveted to the permanent evidence of the moment I'd finally snapped. It had been too late of course, far too late to save my sister. I'd seen the way she'd switched herself off after months of relentless abuse. She had made herself numb to it so he couldn't keep hurting her, though I knew she still felt the pain of his actions. But at least I'd found my courage in the end. Simon was right, he'd pushed me too far, but not for the reasons he'd assumed in his twisted version of reality.

"I didn't blame you, you know. Your passion was always one of your greatest assets. I won't lie. I was scared for a while there. I didn't understand. But I should have known not to underestimate you, you little genius. You knew exactly what you were doing. You wanted to send me a message, didn't you, Belle? But you didn't want to hurt me, not really. You can't imagine how I laughed when the surgeon told me you'd missed every major organ. Clever girl. Just the right amount of pain to make me understand, but you didn't want to hurt me more than you had to. I understand that more than most. I myself have had to make that choice to drill home a point. You went just far enough. And I paid attention. Lying in that hospital bed, I swore to myself that I would never touch your sister again. But that's where it stops making sense. I thought you would come to me. Give yourself to me at last. I was fully prepared to take care of you, be the man you wanted me to be. We were so close, weren't we? So tight, just the two of us? But then I came out of hospital to find you'd all packed up and left. Disappeared like smoke into the night. You let me down, Belle. Why did you do that?"

"I didn't owe you a thing," I spat, though my voice came out shaky and uncertain. I hated the fear that he could put into me. The smile slipped from his face and he took a step forward, ignoring the wave of the knife in my hand.

"I didn't think you had it in you, to betray Bonnie the way you did."

"Betray? The only betrayal was my not standing up for her sooner."

"So she knows does she? That you filmed me with her?"

I shook my head, my eyes falling to the floor. "You gave me no choice. It was the only way to get rid of you. You know it was."

"You could have just given it straight to the police. Had me sent down for... rape, if that's what you want to call it."

"Not without hurting Bonnie. She didn't want to tell. She never even acknowledged what you did. It would have killed her to have to answer questions, talk about it. I'd already destroyed too much of her to break her trust again. Don't get me wrong, I would have, if we hadn't left. If you'd somehow found us. I wasn't bluffing. But I was glad I didn't have to go that far, for her sake, not yours. I regretted making that choice though. Every single day. Wondering if you were out there, grooming some other child, taking away their innocence without them even realising what you were doing until they were in too deep to get out. I regretted it."

"I don't believe you."

"What?"

"I think you wanted to protect me. Keep me safe. You knew I'd come back for you one day." He leaned against the counter, and I noticed the move brought him closer to where I stood. His body language was casual but it felt forced, fake. He looked at me, his mouth twisting in an ugly sneer as he took in my appearance. "All these years I've never stopped thinking about you. Knowing, *believing* that one day I would get to have you. And now you're here in front of me, it's not what I hoped. You've grown old. Jaded. That innocence you had... it's all gone."

"I was a fucking child! A *child,* Simon, do you hear what I'm saying? And now, I'm an adult and you don't want me anymore! Can you even understand what that means? What that makes you? You're sick!"

He looked at me, a slow smile spreading over his face. "I didn't say I don't want you. It would be a shame to wait so long and not find out what I've been missing all these years." I shook my head, my stomach churning as I saw the intent in his eyes. I glanced toward the back door, wondering if I could run. If I could just get outside I could get to Lucas. To safety. But Sophie was still asleep upstairs. I couldn't leave her. Maybe I could get past him, run to her room and barricade the door, somehow? Or next door, just to call the police? My eyes flicked to the back door again. It was locked, but the key was in the door. I just had to turn it to the left and I'd be free. And with any luck, he'd follow me rather than going for Sophie.

Simon seemed to read my thoughts, his smile turning dark, unstable. Without warning, he lunged, grabbing my wrist so hard that the knife slipped from my fingers, clattering loudly to the ground. My back slammed into the counter, the pointed handle on the cutlery drawer jabbing hard into my hip, ripping through my skin, blood trickling down my thigh as he grabbed the back of my hair, pulling me close to his face. "I'd pictured this going somewhat differently. I'd planned to be gentle. But it seems you're more like your sister than I'd hoped."

Chapter Twenty-Nine

His breath was hot against my cheek as he whispered into my ear. My wrists were clamped in his vice like grasp and his body had me pinned. There was no way to escape. "You're going to give me what I want, quietly and willingly," he said softly.

"No!"

"Yes," he hissed, moving so his thigh pressed between my legs, through the thin material of my nightgown. "You will, Belle, I know you will. Because if you don't, I'll go upstairs and take it from that stray little child you've picked up. And I *will* make sure it hurts her."

"You won't lay a hand on my daughter. She's six years old! Even you wouldn't stoop so low!"

"Like I never touched Bonnie?" His lips grazed my throat and I swallowed back bile, screwing my eyes shut. "You're the one calling me a predator. Shall we see if you're right? Do you really want to put me to the test?"

"I *will* kill you."

He shrugged. "Not before I leave her with a memory she'll never forget. Oh, I'll do it, Belle. So, what's it going to be?"

The image of him creeping into Sophie's bedroom by the dim glow of her Shrek and Donkey night-light hit me hard. Suddenly everything became simple. He had removed every other choice. I was aware of the slowing of my frantic heartbeat, the way my breath began to calm as I accepted what I needed to do.

"Okay," I said softly. "I'll do what you want."

A wide grin spread across his face as he leaned back to look me in the eye, one smooth hand coming to cup my chin, though he didn't ease his grip on my other wrist. "Because you want this too. I know you do. You always have." He bit down on his lower lip, his breath coming out in a shudder of need, and it took all my willpower not to start thrashing and fighting again. I tried to smile, but it felt stretched and fake against my skin. "Fuck, Isabel. I've wanted you for so long. I'm going to lose my mind if you make me wait a second longer." He bent forward, pressing a kiss against my collarbone. I didn't let myself feel the revulsion simmering beneath the surface, instead I concentrated on the image of Sophie, my need to protect her. I made myself go soft in his arms, the smell of that familiar aftershave bringing goosepimples to my skin.

Simon moved around me, his mouth trailing across my neck, his grip faltering now as he began to run his hands up and down my body, grasping me possessively. I wished I was wearing thick, protective pyjamas rather than this flimsy cotton nightgown. My eyes fixed on the knife that had fallen to the ground and I felt a surge of hope. If I could only get him to step to the left, it would take just a beat for me to dive down and grab it. I *had* to do it.

I took a breath and feigned a groan of pleasure as his hand grazed my breast through the gauzy cotton. He looked up, a knowing smile on his lips, as if to say, *I told you you wanted me too.* I didn't waste the opportunity. Without daring to think through what I was about to do, I leaned forward, kissing him full on the mouth, my hands going to his hair as I eased him around to the left, away from the knife. He kissed me back hard and I knew that this was the moment.

In one fluid movement I pulled back, breaking the kiss and diving to the ground, hoping to confuse him. I reached the knife, but as I made to roll onto my back, the breath was knocked out of me, Simon's body landing heavily along the length of my back. I thrashed behind me, the knife hitting thin air. He grabbed my wrist slamming my hand into the hard tile. Once, twice, and then with a cry of pain, I finally released the weapon. He pressed the side of my face into the cold tile with one palm, his breath coming hard and fast.

"That was a very silly thing to do, Belle. Very silly indeed." I cried out as he slammed my head into the floor. "You know I didn't want to have to hurt you! Why are you being so difficult?" He yanked my hands up behind my back and I couldn't stop the tears slipping from the corners of my eyes as he squeezed my wrists painfully together. I had failed. He was either going to rape me, or punish me so much worse by hurting Sophie. I was so stupid, I should have just let him do what he wanted. Now

I'd risked my daughter's safety and I was furious at myself for my reckless behaviour.

He was silent for a long time, his body pinning me painfully. Almost a minute passed before he spoke again. "I can't do it to you. I won't take what you won't give me, Belle. I want you to *want* to give yourself to me. That's all I've ever wanted." He eased off me and I sat up, rubbing the pins and needles from my wrists, my eyes following his every movement cautiously. He gave a shrug. "But that doesn't mean I don't have needs." He stood up and I saw that he was still hard, after all that. He was unbelievable. "I need to take care of this, then we can talk."

"W – what?"

He ignored my question, dragging me to my feet and pulling me towards the hallway. He pushed me down beside the radiator and yanked a pack of long cable ties from the inside pocket of his jacket.

Wordlessly, he grasped my hands together securing them to the pipes. The cable ties were too tight, I could feel them cutting into my skin, but my comfort was nowhere near the top of my priorities right now. He stood up, and cold fear filled me as he turned toward the stairs. I tried to lurch to my feet, but fell back, my skin burning from the confines of the bonds.

"Simon, no! No, please, wait!" He paused, his foot already on the bottom step. "Please! Please, just come back!"

"Why?"

"Please!" I begged, tears stinging my eyes. I twisted so I was resting on my knees, knowing how pitiful I must look, and not even caring. It was far too late for my pride to matter now. "I'm sorry, okay. I don't know, I just... I panicked. It felt all wrong to just do it on the kitchen side after all this time. I was scared okay. It's not easy for me to give in to this... to you."

He sneered, disbelieving, but he took a step backwards, turning to face me, though his hand still rested on the banister. "You tried to stab me because you were scared? Come on, Belle! You know I've always had an abundance of patience when it comes to you and your sensitive nature, but you must think I'm an idiot if you think I'm going to fall for that crap."

I shook my head, wishing I could reach my face to wipe away the salty tears. "I don't think you're an idiot," I whispered. "It's me who's stupid." I looked up at him, knowing that he would see the little girl I'd once been, the childlike trust that had drawn him to me.

"What do you mean?" His voice was still hard, accusing, but I didn't miss the softening in his eyes. The way he took another small step away from where Sophie slept and closer to me.

I looked down at the ground, his black, shiny shoes filling my vision. "I can't say it. I can't talk about this."

"Talk."

I stayed silent.

"Talk, Isabel. Now."

I sighed, my wrists throbbing as I focused my gaze on those awful shoes. "You *know*," I said softly. "You've always known how I feel. But that doesn't change the fact that it's wrong. It's sick, you and me. You were my mum's boyfriend. And then, the way you treated Bonnie... what you did to her, is it any wonder I fought my feelings for you? It's sick, Simon! Just the idea of it – I'm sick for wanting this. For even thinking I could be with you."

He stood silently, taking in my words, the house silent save for the sound of his heavy breathing and my thumping heartbeat. Then without warning, he closed the gap between us, lowering to his haunches in front of me. His voice was rough, full of emotion as he spoke. "So that's the reason? You've held back all this time out of *guilt*?" I nodded, not meeting his eyes. He threw back his head and laughed so loudly I feared he would wake Sophie. "You silly, sweet girl," he breathed. "I should have known. You're so good. You always were, Belle. My precious, sweet Belle." He wiped the tears from my cheeks and I forced myself to stay still, not to flinch away from his touch. Instead I looked up at him with a small smile. He grinned back. "You don't have to feel guilty. None of this was ever in your control. It just *is*, sweetheart. It's always been there, from the very start. We can't help the way we feel, can we?"

"No," I whispered.

"And you can't keep fighting it. Pretending I'm the enemy. I'm not, darling. I will never be your enemy, *never*." His hands slid down my shoulders and I held my breath as he moved to the ties at my wrists. He gave a little wink. "I think we'll lose these for now. Might be fun sometime though." He pulled a bunch of keys from his pocket. A tiny pair of scissors hung from a keyring, the kind you'd get from a Christmas cracker. I couldn't picture him sitting around a table, eating Christmas dinner, pulling crackers with other laughing, happy people. The whole scene was too fake to accept. I wondered how he'd got them. I swallowed as he snipped my bonds, the blood rushing painfully back into my hands. He pulled me gently to my feet. "I think it's time we stopped playing games with each other. You know what I want."

"Yes." I swallowed again. My throat felt like it was closing, my tongue dry and papery against the roof of my mouth. "Can... can we go to my room?"

"Anywhere, Belle. I don't care."

I smiled. "Come on then." I walked towards the

stairs, my eyes travelling over the vase on the shabby chic hall table, a collection of tulips Sophie had chosen at the market filling it, their purples, pinks and yellows like magnets to her. She loved colour and bright things and nature, it all made her so happy. And if she was happy, I was too. Simon followed closely behind me and I kept my hands hidden, sure that he would spot how much they were trembling. My bare-feet were heavy on the stairs, fear filling every inch of me, my nerves jangling at the knowledge of what I had to do now. I knew it could go horribly wrong. I could get badly hurt and so could Sophie, but I was out of options. If I had to risk myself to save her, I would do it a thousand times over.

Two thirds of the way up with Simon on the step below me, I moved without warning. With the full force of my weight, I threw myself backwards, slamming into him, knocking him off balance. He gave a grunt, the wind thrust out of him and I felt a jolt of satisfaction as he was shoved off the step. The two of us fell backwards with such a force that we barely grazed the stairs, his back slamming into the hardwood floor below, my body whacking into his chest and rolling to the floor in a heap beside him. I was winded and bruised, but I didn't have time to think about any of that. I spun around, clambering to sit on his chest, seeing the way he stared up, shocked, his eyes slightly unfocused. He'd hit his head. *Good.* My blood felt like it was on fire, rage pouring through me. I grabbed the vase, scattering tulips and water everywhere, and slammed it to the ground, breaking it into a thousand pieces. I cast around frantically as I searched for what I needed. One big shard. It glinted up from the polished wooden floorboard, and without stopping to think, I grabbed it in my palm, feeling the sharpness as it cut into my skin.

Simon looked up at me in confusion. "Belle?"

"I'm not your fucking Belle. I never was and I never will be." I saw his eyes darken, anger flashing across his face but I didn't give him an opportunity to move, to punish me. With every ounce of my strength, I rammed the wedge of broken glass into his throat and watched in satisfaction as his eyes opened wide, the blood spilling from his mouth, trickling down his cheek as he grasped wildly for his neck. I batted his hands aside and pushed the glass deeper, twisting it from side to side before yanking it out and jumping back. His eyes rolled, a gurgle emerged from between his blood coated lips and then at last, his head rolled to the side and his eyes fluttered shut. He was dead.

Chapter Thirty

I don't know how long I sat at the bottom of the stairs, head in hands, unable to tear my eyes up to look at the body strewn across the floorboards. I couldn't stop shaking, the smell of the congealing blood bringing the burning taste of bile to the back of my throat. I had done it again. I'd killed someone. Now there was no passing it off as a one off response, a desperate woman reacting to being cornered. Though that was the perfect truth, it wouldn't matter. The police wouldn't believe it, not this time. And I knew without a doubt that if I called them now, it would set off a chain of events I would live to regret. They would begin to dig. They'd look at my last arrest, David's death, and if they searched hard enough, they would find a reason to take me away forever.

Every single thing I'd done was for Sophie. I believed that with all my heart. Yet, I didn't know who I'd become in the past month. It was impossible to understand how a woman who found it so simple to decide her only choice was murder, could be the same person who'd cried hysterically when she'd not been given extra homework over the summer holidays as a child. The loving mother who'd sung her daughter to sleep every night since she'd brought her home. I *knew* I could be a good person, but now I had done things I had never believed were possible for someone like me. I'd changed into someone I couldn't even recognise.

Part of me wished I could fall to my knees and sob, filled with regret for my actions, but the truth was, I didn't regret killing Simon. Not one bit. I had done what I needed to do to protect my child, and given the same circumstances, I would make the very same choice again. He should have known never to threaten a mother's child. He'd pushed me too far.

Coming to my senses, I stood up, taking a breath and wiping my blood stained hands across my nightgown. The white cotton was streaked with rusty patches of drying blood and I avoided my reflection in the half length mirror which hung on the wall beside the sitting room door. I didn't want to see. Stripping it off, I dumped the ruined nightgown over Simon's body, making sure it covered his face so that I wouldn't have to look at him, and walked to the kitchen, treading carefully so as to avoid the wet patches. I ran the tap until the water was scalding, steam billowing as I scrubbed at my hands, my nails, my arms and face until they were clean, though I knew there would still be traces of him there. I could never wash him away completely. I blotted my face with a dry tea towel, then gulped down half a glass of cool water, staring out the window into the blackness of the back garden. I still had five or six hours of darkness left, but I needed to act quickly. This mess needed to be gone long before Sophie woke up.

I tiptoed back down the hall and stepped over the body, never lowering my eyes even for a moment. Feeling the bile begin to rise again at the memory of what I'd done, I swallowed hard, not allowing myself to be drawn into the flashback. I took the stairs two at a time, pausing outside Sophie's bedroom door. No sound came from within, but I knew that meant nothing. She'd been conditioned to stay quiet through years of abuse at the hands of her biological parents. It hadn't seemed to make a difference that I encouraged her to speak up, ask questions, relax in the safety of her own home. Some things were too deeply engrained to ever be undone. No matter what, she would never have dared to come and investigate sounds of violence.

Fearing what I might find behind the closed door, I summoned my courage and prepared to comfort her. Pushing open her bedroom door, I let out a breath of relief. She was lying on her side, facing me, mouth slightly ajar, a tiny trail of dribble tracking it's way across her cheek as she snored gently, safe and contented in sleep. She'd always been a deep sleeper, a fact I lamented often when I had to try and rouse her for school, but tonight I was grateful for it. It had kept her safe.

I pulled the door, quietly closing it again and went to my own room, rifling through my drawers until I found what I was searching for. A long sleeved black hoodie and black tracksuit bottoms. Right at the bottom of my wardrobe was a box. I eased it out and flipped open the lid. Inside sat a pair of charcoal coloured running shoes I'd bought on a whim but never actually worn because they were way too big. Which would work in my favour tonight. Silently, mind whirring like a hummingbirds wings, I dressed and then I rummaged through my bedside cabinet for the old, pay as you go mobile phone I kept for emergencies. I dialled quickly, tapping my free hand nervously against my thigh. The ringing seemed to go on forever. "Pick up. Pick up, pick up, pick up," I repeated, my throat tight. Finally, just as I was losing all hope, the line clicked and a sleepy voice answered.

"Hello?"

"Bonnie," I breathed. "I need you."

Bonnie was paler than I'd ever seen her before. Dressed all in black, just as I'd instructed in my garbled, nonsensical message on the phone, she'd come quickly, not understanding what was happening. She stood now, looking like some anime ninja straight out of a comic book, her auburn hair tucked under a black wooly hat, her wide green eyes staring at the inert lump that laid before her. "Why the fuck didn't you tell me he was back?" she said, her voice hoarse. "Isabel. Why on earth would you keep this to yourself?"

"You know why. I couldn't risk... I didn't want you to – "

"Lose my mind? Well, thanks for that." She stared at me like I was the one falling off the rails, and I could understand why. "You killed him."

"I had to. He was going to..." I shook my head, my eyes beginning to sting. I blinked back the tears and gave a small shrug. "He threatened Sophie."

Bonnie's face froze, her eyes widening. She didn't speak. Slowly, she crouched beside him, her hand moving towards the nightgown as she moved to uncover his face.

"Wait!"

She looked up at me and I held out a pair of gloves. Grey, leather ones. I was already wearing a similar pair in navy blue. I'd bought both pairs on a trip to Harrods over Easter. Lucas and I had taken the kids to see The Lion King and then looked round the shops, where I'd found the gloves on sale and decided to keep them for the winter. I would never wear them now, not after tonight at least. "Put these on," I said, thrusting them at her. "We can't leave fingerprints."

She gave me a look of disdain, but took them anyway, sliding them on to her slender hands. She whipped the nightgown off without ceremony, looking down at him, her expression unreadable. I couldn't bring myself to follow her gaze, I didn't want to see his blood splattered face again. I had enough material to keep me in nightmares for the rest of my life. She didn't speak for a good thirty seconds, and I wondered if she was crying. Then she turned to me, her eyes dry and hard. "You sure he's dead?"

"I stabbed him in the throat."

"That's not what I asked. Look." She pointed to his chest. I followed her gaze. For a moment, nothing happened. Then I saw it. A slow, shallow rise and fall. "He's not dead, Issy."

"But, how can he not be? Look at the blood!" Bonnie shrugged, almost nonchalantly. "What do we do?" I asked, terror filling me. "We should tie his hands. What if he wakes up? He can't wake up!" The panic was beginning to rise in me, but Bonnie was calm.

She gave a wry smile. "Well, we have two choices. We can call for an ambulance, see if they can save him, wait to be arrested and accept the fact that we will never be rid of this man. He took our childhoods from us, and if we save him now, he'll take what's left of our lives too. And they'll take

Sophie into care too."

"No," I whispered.

"Or," she continued. "We can end this now and move on. We can finally get the closure we've always needed."

I nodded. She was right. It was that simple. Save him and sacrifice ourselves, or finish what he started and end this now. Leave him in the past, a bad memory but never again a threat to us. Or to Sophie. "Yes," I said, fixing her with a determined stare. "That's what we have to do."

She clicked her tongue, and gave a short nod. Then, she leaned forward. I could feel the hate pouring from her, a blaze of revenge in her emerald eyes, the months of repression, being quiet and doing what he wanted, it all streamed from her in a torrent of emotion. She bent towards his ear, and I saw her lips moving as she whispered something meant just for him. Her mouth was inches from his blood encrusted skin, but she didn't seen phased by it. Perhaps it was something she'd had enough time to imagine over the years. I knew she had never forgiven him. How could she? My heart pounded, my palms sweating inside the thick gloves as I watched him now. I had to be ready, I needed to act fast if he began to stir.

Bonnie's lips were moving fast as she spoke her final words of victory and I was glad I couldn't hear what she was saying. I didn't want to know. My inaction as a teenager, turning a blind eye to him raping her made me equally guilty for her pain and suffering. I would never ever be able to forgive myself for what I'd let happen. What I'd ignored. Whatever she was whispering to him now, those words of hatred and anger, would have been more than I could bear to hear. I didn't need to be provoked into guilt. I lived with it constantly. And yet I shared in her hatred too. Simon had hurt me by hurting her. He had stolen my childhood too, broken my trust and turned my love for him into something sick and twisted. He had tried to tear Bonnie and I apart, but he'd never succeeded. I almost couldn't bear to watch her crouching over him, but I had to. We were in this together, as we'd always been. The two of us and him. And now we were no longer his puppets to play against one another. He couldn't hurt us anymore.

Bonnie finished whispering and sat up suddenly. She didn't look back at me for my approval. I could see it didn't matter to her now. Her mind was made up. Her small hands snaked their way around the blood encrusted surface of his neck. And then, she was squeezing as hard as she could, her body shuddering with the exertion of it, her eyes wide as she watched the life seep out of him. His chest rose and fell, rose and fell and then finally stilled, yet Bonnie didn't let go. She continued to squeeze, long after he was dead. "Bon," I whispered softly, touching her lightly on the shoulder. "He's gone, sweetheart."

She gave a final grunt then fell back, breathless and shaking. When she looked up at me I was terrified at what I saw in her eyes. They were empty and flat. I had known this might push her too far. If there had been any way not to call her, I would have chosen it, but I couldn't have finished this on my own. "Are you alright?" I asked, crouching down to her level. It seemed a strange question to ask, given the circumstances and I shook my head, disappointed in myself for saying something so stupid. *Of course she wasn't alright.* But as she caught her breath, I watched the hardness leave her face, relief passing over her.

"That was the easy part," she said. "Now, we have to get rid of him."

Chapter Thirty-One

"I cannot believe I let you talk me into this!"

"What!" Bonnie whispered sharply. "Are you joking? You called me!"

"Shut up and lift."

She grunted and I threw nervous glances over my shoulder as we positioned ourselves beside the car boot, trying to heave the body into it. If someone had told me yesterday that I would be slogging a dead body wrapped in bin-bags into the boot of my car in the dead of the night, I would have thought they were crazy, but here we were. It seemed that both Bonnie and I were at our best when faced with extreme pressure and a deadline. It had been like we'd switched off any emotions that might try to get in the way as we came up with a plan and then began to execute it right away. We'd stripped Simon naked, putting his clothes in one bin-bag, my nightgown in another. We'd washed his hands, cut his nails, poured bleach over his hair and face to kill any traces of ourselves, though I wasn't sure if that was effective or just something I'd seen in a film. After we'd wrapped him in black bin-bags and taped them shut with masking tape, I'd gone to check on Sophie again and come back to find Bonnie with the TV remote in her hand, no longer wearing her hat or gloves.

"What are you doing!"

"Ordering a film."

I'd stared at her blankly, wondering if she'd cracked. "Bonnie..."

"Alibi!" she said, shaking her head as if I were stupid. "We needed a girls night. We watched a movie. We ate popcorn," she pointed to the bowl on the table and the half empty bottle of wine. "I stayed the night after falling asleep on the sofa. Come here." I walked towards her, wordlessly. She pulled the hat from my head and put it beside hers on the table, running her hands through my hair to bring some volume back to it. "Gloves too," she said, waiting patiently as I pulled them off. She guided me down on the sofa and wrapped a rainbow coloured crochet blanket around both of us, covering our cat burglar attire.

"What are you – "

"Shush. Hold this and smile." She placed a glass of red wine in my hand and picked up her phone, then kissed me on the cheek, snapping a selfie. It looked like the perfect picture of happiness. She bent her head low, her fingers flying over the phone screen, then held it up to show me the post she'd made on Facebook as the opening music from The Notebook started playing softly in the background.

Girly all nighter with my besty. Film, wine, and

gossip, what's not to love? (other than the hangover in the morning!) ;)

"Right. Good idea," I nodded, feeling like we'd just invited the world into our secret. "Sophie's still asleep. She shouldn't wake up, but it feels wrong to leave her alone in bed."

"We don't have a choice. Let's just do this as quickly as possible. You know where we're going?"

"Yes." I pulled on the hat and handed hers back to her.

I'd backed the car up as close as I could manage to the front door, but still, we were one eight stone and one seven stone women, neither of whom had ever set foot in a gym, attempting to maneuver a six foot man. Simon was tall, broad shouldered and muscular, and the bin-bags were slippery to hold. "Don't let it rip," I whispered sharply as Bonnie's grip faltered.

"I didn't."

"Good. Don't." With a colossal effort, we managed to swing the bound body into the boot, where I'd laid even more bin-bags in preparation. We both straightened instantly, staring up and down the deserted street, looking up at the neighbours darkened windows to see if anyone was watching.

"We're good. Let's go," Bonnie said. I locked the front door, hoping Sophie wouldn't wake and find me gone, and got into the drivers seat, heart pounding. Bonnie slipped into the passenger seat beside me, her gloved hands clasped tightly together. I was glad I was driving, I needed to keep doing something, to feel like I was moving. Staying still would be torture right now. We drove through the darkened streets, away from the built up areas of houses and shops and into the countryside. My breathing slowed as we wound our way down little lanes, the unlit roads making me feel safer under their blanket of darkness.

"It's just up here," I said, my low voice seeming harsh and jarring in the quiet of the car. I drove along the bumpy, untarmacked lane until the river came into view. "Do you remember coming here?"

"Yes," Bonnie said quietly. "With Roxy and Mum. Not long after we left Bath."

"She wanted to take us for a family day out. A picnic. All four of us together. Like we could start afresh, pretend none of it had ever happened."

"I remember. It was too little, too late."

"I know."

I pulled the car up beside the River Thames, it's inky surface shining in the starlight. I hadn't picked this spot out of any sense of sentimentality, not really. I'd chosen it because there was a sharp drop off from the side, and the river was deep, even right at the edge. There were no banks here for him to wash up. Bonnie and I looked at each other and got to work without a word. We heaved him out of the boot, Bonnie climbing inside to push him as I pulled backwards. He fell to the ground with a thump. We collected the bags we'd used to line the boot and slid them over his already wrapped body. Then, without stopping to discuss it, we picked up rocks and stones from the ground, filling the bags with them and taping them closed around him. I grabbed his head and she went for the feet. It seemed easier to lift him now, the adrenaline rushing through me, the end in sight. We lifted him towards the drop off and with a final look at each other, we swung him into the murky waters, watching with relief and satisfaction as his body bobbed on the surface for a moment before disappearing under. We waited, hand in hand to see if he'd come back up, but he didn't. It had worked.

In silence, we drove back down the lane, and further away from town, stopping to burn the bag of his clothes on the edge of a field, and then fifteen minutes later, we pulled up at another secluded spot by the river to burn my nightgown and everything we were wearing. We changed into the clean clothes I had packed in the back of the car, the air heavy around us as we went through everything in low voices, making sure we'd not missed a scrap of evidence. Bonnie was just about to get back in the car when I stopped her. "Wait!" She turned expectantly. "One last thing." I leaned past her, reaching into the glove box in the car and pulled out the jewellery box Simon had sent me. I'd stashed it in there after lining the boot, and very nearly forgotten about it. I opened it, showing the heart shaped locket to Bonnie and she gave a scoff.

"Pretty," she smirked.

"After all this time, he still believed that what he did was out of love for me." I shook my head. "I think he really believed that, Bonnie. In that twisted mind of his, this was what love looked like."

"And what about you? You loved him once, didn't you?" she asked, catching me off guard. "That's why you found it so hard to believe he wasn't who you wanted him to be."

I gave a short nod. "Yes. I loved him, but as a father. That went up in smoke the moment I realised who he was. He ruined it," I said softly, looking down at the necklace. "Bonnie. I've never said it, and I know there have been plenty of opportunities, but I never took them. But I have to say it now. This won't be over until I do."

"Say what?"

"I'm sorry. I'm so fucking sorry I didn't stop him. I'm sorry I let him hurt you," I said, letting my tears fall freely without fighting against them for once. "I hate myself for not having had the courage to do something. I'm just as much to blame for what you've been through as he is."

She stepped forward, her hands grasping my

shoulders tightly. "Don't you dare say that, Issy. It's not true. You were a *child*. So much more innocent than I was at that age, with your books and your homework and exams. You spent so much time thinking about your schoolwork, you were sheltered from the world I lived in. You know that."

"It's not an excuse, Bonnie. I still knew right from wrong."

"So did he. You were scared and confused and he took advantage of both of us, whether he touched you or not. I was jealous of you at the time, of course. I wished I could be the special one instead of you. The one he worshipped rather than used. I thought it might be easier. But now I know, you had it just as hard as I did. I know he made you think it was your fault, the way he treated me. He was trying to make you say yes to him. I don't blame you, Issy. I love you. I always have."

"You don't hate me?"

"Never."

"I hate myself."

She shook her head. "You're a good person whose been put in shitty situations. Look at everything you've done for Sophie."

"Not as much as she's done for me. She's given me a purpose."

"She's brought out the best in you. He brought out the worst."

I leaned into her, and she hugged me back tightly, her own tears damp against my shoulder. "You're right," I said softly, pulling back to look at her. "And we can't let him influence our lives anymore. He's taken so much from us already."

"Good riddance," Bonnie said as I turned towards the river.

I took one final look at the necklace. "Goodbye, Simon. You can't hurt us now," I whispered into the darkness. Then I launched it, box and all into the river. There was a splash as it landed and then I lost sight of it in the black water.

"Let's get back, Bonnie said, taking my arm and leading me to the car. "It's finished."

"I hope you're right."

"I'm always right," she smiled.

Chapter Thirty-Two

The clock chimed 5 a.m. as I snuggled under a fleecy blanket on the sofa, holding the generous glass of wine Bonnie had poured for me. We'd parked in my usual spot on the driveway, bleached the floors and the sink, wiped down every surface and handle in the house and Sophie had slept through the entire thing. I would never get annoyed by her inability to wake for school again. Now we were too wired to sleep, and neither of us wanted to be alone.

"So now I guess I know everything," Bonnie said sipping her wine.

I looked at her, then ran my fingers along the seam of a cushion, realising I had a chance to tell someone what I'd been holding back all these weeks. "Not quite."

"What do you mean, *not quite?*"

I looked up at her, seeing the mirror image of myself, my other half, the one person who knew everything I'd been through, who had shared in all my traumas. "I murdered David Harrison," I said, looking her right in the eye. Bonnie stared at me wordlessly, her expression analysing rather than judging.

"You killed him, yes. In self defence. That isn't the same as murder, Issy." I shook my head and her eyes narrowed. "Isabel, the two of us are tied together with so many secrets, a tangled web of the stories we can never share with anyone else. The things we've been through, what we've done... what's one more revelation between sisters?" She reached across the sofa, linking her fingers through mine. "We've both done terrible things. Tell me the truth. Trust me to keep your secrets as you have mine all this time." She squeezed my hand. "What happened with David, Issy?"

I looked down at my lap, my fingers shaking at the rawness of our situation, the words that I knew had to come out before they made me explode with the pressure of holding them in. "Some of what I told you was the truth. David did work for me, but it was for longer than two weeks. His dad ran the family business, but David was trying to break off on his own, pick up clients for himself, so he spent the day working for his dad and then in the evenings he took on other clients. I was one of them. I told the police he'd only been coming when we were out, but that was a lie. For a month, he came over every night. He was friendly. I thought he seemed decent. He had dinner a few times with me and Sophie."

"And nobody knew?"

"No. He didn't want his dad to find out. I paid

him cash, and there was no trace of him working here. I worried when I first told the police, you know, that his dad would tell them I was lying, that he couldn't have come to me in the daytime because he was working with him somewhere else, but then I remembered David saying that his dad had been in the hospital for five weeks with his heart, so he wouldn't have known, would he? I should have been more careful with my story though, that could have messed everything up."

"So, what happened? Did you fall for him? You were spending all those evenings together – "

"No, nothing like that." I sighed and took a gulp of my wine. "I got too relaxed. Too used to having him around. We have a routine, you know? Every night after school Sophie goes to her room to play with her toys and I cook dinner. David was supposed to be painting the bathroom, tiling, fixing that leaky tap. He was supposed to be busy..."

"Isabel... he didn't... Sophie?" she whispered, leaning forward as the pieces tried to match up in her mind. Her eyes were wide and frightened.

"No." I saw the breath leave her as her hands unfurled from the tightly balled fists she'd been holding to her mouth. She pressed the tips of her fingers together, tapping them nervously against her chin as if sending out a silent prayer. Swallowing, I looked back to my lap, my nails working at a loose thread on the cushion, creating a hole. I didn't care, I couldn't stop. "I went to see her in her room that night... the night it happened. You know what she's been through, the violence her biological dad inflicted on her. Ever since she's been with me we've talked so much about keeping safe. About the danger of keeping secrets, and how she needs to be open with me about everything so I can always help her. Protect her. It's become a habit for her. She literally tells me everything. I don't think she even realised what she'd said, the significance of what it meant."

"What? What did she tell you, Issy?"

"David was downstairs, getting ready to leave. He'd only come round to put up a shelf for me under the mirror in the bathroom, just a quick job. I'd popped in to tell Sophie dinner was going to be late... she was playing with her baby dolls," I paused. Now was the time to stop. If I carried on, there would be no turning back. I took a breath. "She was just chatting away like always. She said she had a friend, he played with her every day and sometimes he kissed her... on the lips. I thought she meant a boy at school, her first crush or something. She's only six! So I asked if he was in her class, and she started laughing." Tears sprang to my eyes as I remembered the sweet look of innocence on her little face, her eyes wide and sparkling. "She said, *no silly Mummy! It's David!*"

Bonnie grabbed my hand again, squeezing tightly, her teeth biting down on her lower lip hard enough to draw blood. She remained silent so I continued, not daring to look her in the eye. "I checked. I promise, I did. I said, *do you mean the handyman, David, sweetie? The man downstairs?* And she said yes. She said she was glad he was going to keep working for us, because he'd promised her they could have a sleepover, that he had a magic key to come and visit her at night-time and they could have a midnight feast... and then... then she said, when he'd kissed her goodbye..." the words came out as a strangled mass as the sobs began to rock through my body.

"Issy?"

"She said that... when he kissed her, his tongue accidentally went inside her mouth and touched hers. She thought it was funny, Bonnie!"

"Oh my god."

I looked up at her, tears streaming down both of our faces, blurring everything. "I let you down, Bonnie. I know I did. Every time he came into our room at night, every time he... he..."

"Raped me."

I nodded. "Yes. I should have done something. I should have stopped him. But I was too afraid."

"You did something in the end, Issy. You stabbed him in the chest. You made him have to go to hospital, gave us all a chance to escape and start again."

"It was too late. The damage was already done."

"It's never too late. It could have carried on for years!"

I wiped at my eyes, remembering how I'd felt when I realised Sophie was being groomed by another man I'd been stupid enough to trust. "When she told me... I just snapped, Bon. I told her to keep playing her game, acted like everything was totally normal, and then I went downstairs to the kitchen, picked up the biggest knife from the block and stabbed him as hard as I could. He didn't even see it coming. I didn't say a word, but he knew why. I know he did. I messed up with Simon. How can you stab someone in the chest and miss everything that matters? But this time, I wasn't some scared little girl lashing out in confusion. I knew exactly what I was doing. I stabbed him right in the heart, pulled the knife out and waited for him to bleed out before I called the police. I'd do it again in a second if it meant keeping her safe. I don't regret it, Bonnie, but I won't go to prison for it. I won't abandon my child because I took the life of someone like him. Do you hate me?"

"No. I would have done the same. I did do the same tonight, didn't I? Only I wish I'd done it a lot sooner. So we're both murderers."

"I suppose so."

"But they gave us no choice." Bonnie leaned forward, grabbing the half full bottle of wine from the table, pouring generous measures into both of our glasses. "How do you feel now that you've told me?"

I thought about it for a second. "I feel free."

"Me too. I feel like I can breathe now I know Simon's not ever coming back."

"Nobody can ever know, Bonnie. No one can ever find out what we did."

"They won't."

"Bonnie... you can't let go of reality anymore. You can't give in to the Bipolar. If you do, this will all come out. You have to promise me you'll take your meds. You'll keep turning up to get those injections. You'll get help the moment things feel wrong. We have too much to risk. Come to me, okay? If you feel yourself slipping."

"You know what made me want to keep

disappearing into that blissful oblivion? The knowledge that he would come back for me. That he was out there biding his time. I've been stuck in my thirteen year old fears all my adult life, I've never stopped trying to run from him. But now, he's gone. Forever. And I honestly believe I can begin to heal now. I can let him go to hell. I won't let you down with this, Issy. I get what it would mean for you. For Sophie."

"Thank you," I whispered, hugging her tight against me. "And I'm sorry. For everything."

"Me too," she said into my hair. "Secrets between sisters remain secrets forever." She pulled back and clinked her glass against mine in a morbid kind of toast, and then we were both laughing and sobbing and hugging again as we let out all the pain we'd held in our hearts for so long. It was all going to be okay.

Epilogue

Ten days later

"I shouldn't be doing this!"

"Isabel."

"I'm serious. I'm too old for all this."

"Oh shut up. If you're too old, that makes me too old and I'm only just getting started. Tell me honestly, are your instincts screaming no, or are you just nervous?"

I bit my lip, staring at my made up reflection in the mirror above my dresser. "Nervous. Terrified. All of that."

"But it's a good fear," Bonnie smiled triumphantly. "The start of something new, something exciting. So you're bloody going to do it."

I sighed. "I knew getting you round was a bad idea." She leaned back on the bed, a mug of tea clasped in her hands.

"You look fantastic."

"Ha! You would say that."

"Auntie Bonnie!" Sophie rushed into the room and jumped onto the bed, making the springs creak ominously. I winced as Bonnie's tea sloshed over the side of her cup onto my Egyptian cotton sheets, but held my tongue. Bonnie wrapped an arm round Sophie's shoulder and the two of them leaned into each other, making my heart soar. They looked happy. At peace, and somehow a little tea stain didn't seem to matter anymore. "Mummy, you look so pretty," Sophie said, watching me as I clasped a small silver pendant around my neck.

"Do I? Thank you sweetie."

The doorbell rang, and Sophie squealed in delight! "They're here!" She jumped off the bed and ran out of the room. I swallowed and suddenly Bonnie was at my shoulder, her eyes meeting mine in the mirror.

"Let yourself have this," she said quietly, her lips beside my ear. "She would have wanted it. You've punished yourself enough, Issy. It's time you started living. Taking something for yourself." My eyes stung with hot tears and I blinked them back, nodding wordlessly. I hugged her tightly, reluctant to let go, but she released me, turning me to face the bedroom door. "Go," she grinned. "What are you waiting for?" I took a deep breath and nodded, then went downstairs. I opened the front door, Sophie jumping around my ankles like a hyper puppy. Oscar was like a bolt of lightening as he whizzed into the house, whooping in delight.

"You're going to sleep in my room, Oscar!"

Sophie yelled, grabbing him by the shoulders and bouncing up and down. "And Auntie Bonnie said we could have as many Disney films and sweets as we want!"

"Did she now?" I said, raising an eyebrow, but they were already running upstairs to where Bonnie had laid out a carpet picnic for the three of them. I turned slowly, awkward now. Lucas stood there in a beautifully cut dark blue suit, his crisp white shirt open at the collar, freshly shaven and smelling delicious. It had been a long time, years in fact, since I'd seen him like this.

"Hi," he said softly.

"Hi."

"You sure they won't be too much for Bonnie?"

I shook my head. "No. She can handle them. She can handle a lot more than we give her credit for. She's doing well."

He nodded. He was nervous too, I realised. "I

didn't think you would … I didn't know if..."

I bowed my head. "I know. I'm sorry it took me so long to call. And that we didn't get a chance to talk properly after... after we got close," I lifted my eyes to meet his. "Things were all messed up after David. All that stuff with his family. And I was really confused. About Roxy. How she'd feel, you know?"

"That's understandable. I was too for a while."

"But not now?"

"No." He grinned at me and I felt myself relax. "I'm glad you called. This was a good idea, it's been years since I've been asked out on a date."

With Roxy. But Bonnie was right. She would have been so happy to know that Lucas and I were growing closer. Falling for each other, even. And the world of dating was pretty foreign territory for me too. I couldn't think of anyone I'd rather be going out with. I grabbed my coat off the banister pulling it on, and called out goodbye to Bonnie who was purposefully avoiding us to give us our moment. "So, dinner?" I said with a shaky smile.

"Dinner."

"Right then."

I stepped out into the cool night air and felt his big, warm hand wrap around mine as we began the short walk to the little Italian restaurant I'd chosen. It felt natural. Right. And maybe it was okay that I had secrets I'd never be able to share with him. After all, every couple had things hidden in the shadows between them, stories they'd prefer not to tell. Maybe we could survive, despite it all. I squeezed his hand tightly, filled with hope and excitement as together we walked towards a second chance for the both of us.

The end.

About This Story

When I finished writing One More Tomorrow, the book set six years prior to Keep it Secret, I knew I had unfinished business with Isabel and Bonnie. Right from the start, I knew Isabel was hiding some deep, dark secrets, covering them with the heroic, put together front she presented to the world.

The first scene I wrote for Keep it Secret was the scene in which Simon crawls into the twins' bed and rapes Bonnie, though it's written in a way that makes you think it could be Isabel. I planned to reveal the truth, that it was in fact Bonnie who was abused, much closer to the end. However, as is normally the way when writing a book, the characters had other ideas! I feel like these characters have worked their way under my skin and I may well revisit them again in the future.

The story with David came to me out of the blue when I was home alone with my two young children. I was washing up at the sink after lunch and realised I couldn't hear them playing, and suddenly my imagination went wild imagining what I might do if someone broke in and tried to take them or attack me while they were playing upstairs. How a person might be capable of killing if their children's safety was at stake. David was always going to be a story of Isabel reacting in self defence, but I realised the potential for a darker backstory and the cover up of the perfect murder as the novel came together.

The subject matter was fairly gritty to write, and I hope for those who have been groomed themselves, I did it justice. I debated with myself about having Isabel become a double murderer, after all, most people would choose to go to the police in her situation, and I wondered if it might make her an unlikeable protagonist, but then, my goal was not to make her into what she *should* be, but rather to show just how broken she had been by her childhood experiences, and how, when pushed, her instinct was to choose the most extreme solution to solve her problems. My goal is not to judge the actions of my characters, but to tell them as they are and have *you*, the reader decide on whether or not she was justified. Isabel in my mind has always been a compulsive secret keeper and it felt very apt to have her finish her story without a clean slate.

What did you think? I hope you enjoyed reading the story and I would be so grateful if you could leave a review. They make such a huge difference to how well my books sell, and help other readers to discover them.

If you would like to be notified when I release something new, and take advantage of my launch discount prices, come and join my reader list at www.SamVickery.com.

Lots of Love,

Sam

Also by Sam Vickery

The Promise

Available on Amazon worldwide

Chapter One

Emily leaned over the tiny stainless steel sink, pulling her long black hair to one side and holding it in place as she bent forward to wash her face. The water splashed down onto the dark haired baby she wore strapped to her chest, and he squealed nuzzling his cheek into her cardigan, rubbing the moisture away. She winced as the icy water turned her fingertips blue, and reached over to the soap dispenser only to find it empty. Again.

Sighing, she took a handful of paper towels and rubbed the rough surface over her skin until she was dry. She took one more and held it under the trickling tap, then squeezed it in her fingers, watching the excess water filter away. She leaned forward, dangling the baby backwards so that she could reach his face, and deftly used the damp paper to clean his skin.

He arched away and she dipped into the woven wrap, locating a sticky hand and pulling it free. She cleaned it thoroughly and then found the other one. "No need to look so worried Flynn," she muttered. "It's way to cold for a big wash, you're getting away with the bare minimum today, lucky boy!"

She tossed the paper towel into the bin and grabbed her backpack, slinging the heavy weight onto her shoulders. Loud, happy voices echoed through the public toilets, and Emily looked behind her to see two women entering, one blonde and soft looking, one pixie like redhead, both pushing buggies overladen with changing bags and souvenirs. Emily immediately spotted a plastic bag with the Natural History Museum logo on it and smiled widely. Jackpot.

Without a doubt, the best thing about being homeless in London was the tourists. They never failed to surprise her with their sheer naivety.

Stealing from them, conning them in some way or another, it was almost too simple. But Emily didn't crave challenge, she didn't wish they would make it a little harder to get what she wanted. What she craved was food. Money to buy clothes for her growing son, safety. Day to day life was challenging enough. The easy tourists were a gift and she hoped these two wouldn't let her down.

Emily smiled confidently at them and pushed her numerous fake gold and silver bangles up her forearm, pointing to the two sleeping toddlers in their buggies. "Long day?" she asked.

"Yes," the blonde woman sighed happily. "We've seen everything. They've had so much fun!"

"How old are they?"

"Both two. This is Thomas," she said, pointing to the red cheeked, blonde haired boy in front of her. "And this is Elizabeth," she gestured to her friend's child. "How old is yours?"

Emily looked down at her son, smiling with pride. "He's ten months."

"You're not wearing any shoes," the pixie

woman exclaimed, noticing the dirty bare feet poking out from beneath her flowing skirt. "Is this a new fashion thing? You must be freezing!"

"Uh, no, not a fashion thing. More a stepped in a big puddle thing. They're in my bag. I was just going to go and get some new ones for the journey home," she lied, not wanting to tell them the truth. That she had swapped her shoes last week for a BLT and a Starbucks latte with "Woozy Susie." It had been getting dark and Emily hadn't eaten all day, when Susie, a no nonsense, afro haired, pickled livered, sixty year old woman who had been on the streets most her life, had struck up the deal with her. She had been too hungry to even think of saying no.

For some reason, and she couldn't fathom why, she got a lot less charity than others in the area. You would think that with a baby, people would be falling over themselves to help her, but it wasn't like that. If anything, they judged her harder and ignored her even more than the standard prescription for the misfortunate. If only they knew what she had been through to end up in this situation. If only they would open their minds for a second and give her a chance to explain.

So, she had no shoes. In October. In London. But she did have a pair of thick woollen socks. She just wasn't about to ruin them walking around the streets in the filth and wet all day, when she could save them and have warm, dry feet tonight.

"I see," the red head said uneasily, breaking eye contact. Emily smiled warmly, and looked away. Her goal was to look wholesome and trustworthy, not an easy thing to accomplish when she was waiting for an opportunity to prove them wrong, but she had been around long enough to know how to play the game. Hell, even before her street life she'd had to hone her skills as an actress.

Pretending. Lying. Trying to keep *him* from seeing the truth, to keep herself safe from his volatile mood swings. She shuddered, not surprised by the sudden turn of her thoughts. She regularly had flashbacks and nightmares, and she thought she saw him at least twice a week. She would be walking along the street and there he would be, striding purposefully towards her. Or sitting on the platform at the train station. Eating a sandwich outside a café.

When that happened, she would melt into the walls, hide her face and hold her breath. She couldn't risk him finding her, finding Flynn. It always took her hours to resume her sense of normality after these false sightings.

But right now, she needed to focus. She glanced over at the women. The pixie was taking a tampon out of her bag, the blonde busily peeling back the blanket from the hot, sleeping child. She needed them to feel comfortable, to see her as just another mother, not as a potential threat. She turned on the water again, making a show of washing her hands. Stalling. The two women parked their buggies beside the sinks and both of them went into the stalls.

Unbelievable, Emily thought, shaking her head. Though she had seen it time and time again, she still couldn't understand what must be going through their minds. To leave not only their belongings, their valuables, but also their precious children right there for the taking in a dirty, public toilet in the middle of London. Emily instinctively wrapped her arms around Flynn, sick at the thought of what could happen if the wrong person saw the unattended children.

Perhaps, she thought introspectively, her fear was a product of her past. Maybe these women had led such blessed lives that they couldn't fathom a time when life would strike them down and leave them ruined. She hoped they would never have to face the consequences of such trusting naivety.

She waited three seconds, wiping her palms dry on her skirt, then walked straight to where the two toddlers were sleeping, completely unaware of the world around them. With expert fingers, she slid a handful of nappies, a packet of wet wipes and one of the two purses from the open bags. She riffled through the purse and found forty pounds in cash.

Grinning, she slipped the now empty purse back into the bag and without hesitating a second longer, walked straight out of the toilets. Forty pound! She felt like jumping up and down with excitement. They would be eating tonight. And she might even splash out and buy some shoes if she could find a cheap pair. She made for the back streets, knowing they would never find her, already pushing their faces from her mind.

She never let herself think about the effect her actions would have on the people she targeted. She couldn't. Yes, it was harsh, yes it would be a little crack in their otherwise perfect day, but she never took credit cards or personal things, and she knew they would manage without it. What would be a nice takeaway or a family day out for them, would mean her and Flynn could eat every day for a fortnight or maybe more. She didn't feel bad taking from them. It was necessary.

Emily could feel the eyes burning into her back as she walked the aisles of the busy supermarket, a basket slung over her arm. She had found a pair of trainers only one size too big for four pounds in the sale bin, and she had made straight for the reduced food section, marked down because it only had a few hours of shelf life left. Four sandwiches marked at thirty pence each and a tub of strawberries for ten pence lay alongside the shoes in her basket. She glanced over her shoulder to see the young, burly security guard following closely behind. This was bullshit. She had money in her pocket and she knew she hadn't done anything wrong.

Emily hated the way people treated her because she was struggling. Homeless. They were scared of her, wary, and she couldn't stand it. This time two years ago she had been shopping in Waitrose, driving a Fiat, a part of society. She had lost everything in the course of one day, but that didn't change who she was deep down. It wasn't fair.

And though she didn't bat an eye at stealing one on one, she would never take the risk of stealing from a real shop. She wouldn't dare, for fear of being hemmed in by security. Of not being able to get out. Of having them take Flynn from her. She was always on her best behaviour in places like this. So why on earth was he following her?

"Miss?"

She turned, a false smile plastered on her face. "Yes?"

"I'm going to have to ask you to leave, if you could just follow me please," the guard said, reaching forward and forcibly taking her basket from her.

"What? Why?"

"You know your kind aren't allowed in here."

"My kind?" she asked, reeling from his insult.

"You know."

"No, I don't. I haven't a clue what you're on about. I just want to buy my food and I'll be going," she said, reaching to take the basket from him.

"Don't make a scene. Come on, let's go."

"No! What have I done? I'm trying to buy food for my son, I haven't done anything wrong!"

"We have enough of you lot coming in here and taking stuff without paying. This ain't a charity love. Go to a soup kitchen or somethin', but don't be coming back here. You ain't welcome."

"I'm not homeless, I'm a backpacker. Fuck. I

didn't do anything wrong, just let me buy the food."

"You ain't got no money, look at you, you don't even have any shoes on and the kids not dressed for this weather," he said, pointing at Flynn's bare feet.

"I'm buying shoes, look!" she shouted, pointing at the basket. "How am I supposed to wear shoes if you won't let me buy them?"

A crowd of curious onlookers was beginning to form at the end of the aisle, though Emily noticed that they kept a safe distance away. Wouldn't want to get too close to the crazy homeless lady now, would they? The guard glanced at them, frowning, then leaned towards Emily, a menacing expression on his face.

"Do I need to call for assistance or are you gonna get out?"

Emily glared at him venomously, hatred burning in her eyes. It wasn't fair. None of this was fair. Every ounce of her wanted to fight this, to stand up for herself and win. But she couldn't risk it. The police would never take her side, that was just the way it went. With an angry grunt, she let go of the basket, her gaze resting briefly on the food she wouldn't get to eat. The shoes she wouldn't get to wear. "Fine. I'll go somewhere else," she said, her fist clenching tightly around the money in her pocket.

With all the dignity she could muster, she turned and walked away, the sound of the crowd's disapproving mutters ringing in her ears. His heavy footsteps followed behind her all the way to the exit.

The Promise is available now on Amazon worldwide.

Printed in Great Britain
by Amazon